MURDER IN MORNINGTON

BY

KEMBERLEE SHORTLAND

A Sassy O'Brien Mystery

Tirgearr Publishing

Published by Tirgearr Publishing
Ireland
www.tirgearrpublishing.com

ISBN 978-1-910234-20-4

A CIP catalogue record for this book is
available from the British Library.

10 9 8 7 6 5 4 3 2 1

DEDICATION

~ Always for Peter ~

ACKNOWLEDGMENTS

I have several people to give thanks to for helping this book mature.

First to my beta readers: Noreen Wainwright, author of the Edith Horton Mysteries; and Elle J. Rossi, author of the Josie Hawk Chronicles. Both of your insights has been invaluable! And extra thanks, Elle, for keeping me from pulling out my hair when things came down to the wire.

Massive thanks goes to Mollie Cox Bryan, author of the Agatha-nominated Cumberland Creek Mysteries, for taking time from her busy schedule to put this book on her reading list, and for her lovely cover quote.

Special thanks go out to a friend in An Garda Siochana, the Irish police force, for his invaluable council on the ins and outs of police procedure in Ireland.

Top marks go to Alicia Stucky for her amazing cover design. Alicia is an amazing illustrator. I'm so fortunate to have her as my designer on this series. When she says, "Your secret is safe with me," you better believe it.

I've had lots of support from family, friends, and readers, and want to thank everyone for helping me through this. This is a new step in my writing career, and an exciting one. Thanks to everyone for taking this journey with me.

Chapter One

The last thing she expected to find while jogging with her dog on Mornington Beach was a body.

A human body.

But there it was. Her breath caught and her stomach tightened.

To be fair, the body wasn't actually on the beach, but on the stony bank along the River Boyne near where it opened into the Irish Sea at Mornington Beach. The river had been an active shipping lane since medieval times for the port town of Drogheda just four miles upriver.

Was he alive? The large man lay on his side with his back to her, so she couldn't tell.

Taking a deep breath, she pulled Bracken to her side and inched closer to the body. The wolfhound strained at the lead, trying to get a sniff between yelps and whines.

The man had shaggy, dark hair and wore a black-wool coat, well-worn, blue denims, and black boots. It seemed to her untrained eye that he could have worked on a ship. Could this man have fallen overboard from one of the ships catching the last high tide? With his damp hair and wet clothes, if he hadn't fallen off a ship, he'd at least been out here since last night's rain.

"Hello?" Her voice squeaked. She took deep breaths, forcing herself to relax. "Are you all right?"

Silence was his only reply.

Her heart pounded in earnest now. The dog's barking didn't help matters, especially where Sassy's shoulders were

1

concerned. Wolfhounds were strong, so even though Bracken was a well-trained dog, it was still a struggle keeping her at heel.

"Whisht. Quiet." She tugged on the lead, and the dog fell in beside her, resorting to soft guttural growls.

Keeping Bracken close, Sassy made a wide arc around the body. The man wasn't moving, so she inched closer and touched his booted foot with her runner-clad toe. "Hey." Still nothing.

She scanned the area for help, but at this hour of the morning, she and Bracken were the only ones about.

Cautiously, she moved in front of him and knelt onto one knee to see if she recognized him beneath the strands of damp hair partially obscuring his face. He didn't look familiar, but he did look pale. Really pale. His lips were grey. She noticed the side of his face was discolored where it rested near the ground, but the rest of him was deathly pale.

Then his lips moved.

He's alive.

She leaned in closer. "I can't hear you. What are you saying? Are you all right?"

Just as she reached out to move aside the hair from his eyes, his mouth opened. What she'd thought was his tongue emerged as a small crab when it spilled onto the ground and skittered away toward the river.

"Oh, dear God!"

Sassy quickly fell back. Bracken's sharp, startled yip meant the dog was behind her, which caused Sassy to lose her balance. She twisted her body, hoping not to crush the poor dog when she landed. Rough stones bit into her hip as she came to a crushing stop, her elbow and shoulder taking the rest of her weight.

Without considering her injuries, she spun onto her back and used her feet to push herself through the stones and away from the dead man. Bracken's lead had wrapped around Sassy's wrist, forcing the dog even closer to her as they moved.

"Jesus, Mary, and Joseph!" Her heart felt like it was going to explode from her chest.

Once more, she gazed around her. This is what she got for running so early in the morning.

She turned her gaze back to the corpse.

She admitted it now. He was a corpse.

Her stomach tensed. She swallowed hard to keep her morning's tea and toast in place.

Buck up. It's just a body. He can't hurt you. It's not like you haven't seen dead people before. Good God, this is Ireland. A good, old-fashioned Irish wake put paid to the fear of seeing dead people. Lots of them. She'd just never seen one on the beach before.

Taking long, deep breaths, Sassy got hold of herself. She pulled her mobile from her coat pocket and dialed 999.

Chapter Two

Her mobile phone rotated in her fingers as her gaze remained on the man. Thoughts spun in her mind. Bracken's grumbling had finally ceased so Sassy could think clearer.

Who was he?

Why was he out there?

How did he get out here . . . or who left him here?

What had happened?

More importantly, *why did I have to be the one who found him?*

Once she'd calmed—a little—she realized she wasn't afraid of him. Dead people can't hurt you. She did feel sorry for him though. Who deserved to die like this?

Though, she had to admit, the scenery was spectacular. Who wouldn't want beauty around them while drawing one's last breath? Here, at the mouth of the Boyne, the Irish Sea with the sunrise on the eastern horizon, the river meandering inland to the west, and the medieval Maiden Tower on the shore, there didn't seem a more picturesque location. Early morning fog still lingered, but she could already tell it would be a beautiful day.

This man wouldn't see it, though, or any other sunrises.

Somehow, she was sure his death had been anything but peaceful.

"Where are the Guards?" The time on her phone meant she'd only called the police five minutes ago but it felt like hours.

She scanned the high line of sea grass on the other side of which was casual parking. Nothing and no one. Except for the gently lapping water, silence filled the air. Too early even for the birds. Even Bracken had laid her head down, though she kept her gaze on the corpse.

Emotions spun through Sassy, from guilt over not being able to help this man, to impatience at waiting for the Guards to arrive.

As the minutes ticked by, her mind relaxed and other thoughts crept in. One of which she wasn't expecting . . . her late-night, guilty pleasure—crime dramas.

Sometimes while watching, she wondered what it would be like to be involved in an investigation. She often guessed who the baddie was almost as soon as the show started.

She was usually right.

But this was reality. This was a real person, and he was really dead.

She was no crime fighter.

Hell, the closest she got to the Guards was driving past the Laytown Garda Station going to and from the main road at Julianstown.

Still . . .

Looking at this man, she paused when Castle popped up in her mind.

What would Beckett do?

A moment later, she brought up the camera app on her mobile and took a couple pictures from where she sat.

"Well, that was dumb." What was she doing taking pictures of a dead man? What was she going to do with them anyway . . . share them on social media? Maybe she should put herself between him and the camera and take a selfie. Her caption: *Me with a dead guy I found on the beach.* She'd be sure to smile real big and give a thumbs up. Yeah, that would impress her family and friends.

"What an eejit!"

Besides, the guards would bring a photographer with

them who was an expert in these things.

She opened the image gallery to delete the photos and stopped. What would Beckett do? kept rolling through her head.

Illogically, her curiosity got the better of her, and she switched back to camera mode.

"Bracken, stay," she commanded. She released her hold on the lead and stood up. With one more look around to confirm she was still on her own, she approached the man, making sure to keep her footprints in the drag marks she'd made moments before when she'd shoved herself away from him. She needed to be sure she left as little of herself at the scene as possible.

Her gaze scanned the stony riverbank for clues . . . a few cigarette butts, a plastic bottle cap, sea glass and shells, strands of seaweed . . . lots of various-sized stones where any number of tiny clues could have fallen between. She took a couple photos around the body then turned her attention to the man himself and scanned the length of him.

Considering the wear, the clothes were actually clean. "Interesting," she muttered while snapping photos from his boots, up his legs, along his back to his head. Then she repeated the process on the front of him. She carefully used the back of her pinky to lift the hair away to snap a picture of his face and the opening of his tightly wrapped jacket.

"Oh, my," she gasped when she spotted blood on his collar. She hadn't even considered *how* he'd died, just that he was dead. Now that she knew what to look for, she noticed there wasn't much blood around him, so it must have pooled under him and seeped into the stones.

Knowing she shouldn't do it, she did it anyway. Using the edge of a broken razor clam she quickly brushed the sand from, she pulled back the collar to examine the blood on his neck. There was a small puncture in his skin that seemed like the source of the blood. It wasn't a big puncture but it looked deep.

Where the collar was protected from the weather, blood had thickened and was drying around the edges. Examining the area, she noticed a small, rectangular piece of dark plastic sticking to the fabric, as if glued in place by the drying blood. She made sure to get a couple pictures of that too. This was definitely a clue. She gave herself a mental pat on the back for the find. It bolstered her confidence, so she carried on.

Next, she gently patted his jacket to see if there was anything in the pockets. The man's arms were partially tucked under him so the jacket was wrapped around him too tightly to feel if there might be a wallet or mobile phone. One or both of those things might reveal his identity, but she wasn't going to disturb the body by digging deeper. The last thing she wanted was the Guards hauling her in for disturbing evidence. It was bad enough what she had already done had probably compromised something.

"What am I doing?"

What Beckett would do?

"I'm not Beckett."

What if you were?

"This is wrong."

There was no logical reason for her to collect photographs and look for evidence. It was one thing to play amateur sleuth while watching Castle . . . or Bones or any of the other dozen crime dramas she watched, but something else entirely when there was a real body in front of you.

She looked over at Bracken, still lying on the riverbank. "What am I doing, Bracken?"

Hearing her name, the dog lifted her massive frame into a sitting position and cocked her head, giving Sassy a look like, "Yeah, what the hell, Mom?" In reality, it was more likely, "Can we go now?" Sassy couldn't agree more.

Where were the Guards anyway?

As she moved to stand, she noticed something clutched in one of the man's hands. "Might as well get a few more. I'll delete them when I get home. Who knows, maybe the Garda photographer won't make it." *Yeah, right.*

Hopefully, by the time the photographer arrived, Sassy would be long gone. Irish investigations ran much differently than those on American television. First, the Guards would come out to make sure she wasn't a crackpot having them out on a wild goose chase, and then when they saw the body, they'd call in the state pathologist. The pathologist would come out with an investigative team, which would include the photographer.

Sassy would be the main witness, since she was the one who discovered the body and called it in. Who knows? She may need these photos if they tried framing her for the murder. Stranger things had happened.

Fear raced through her, and she started shaking again. All she wanted to do was run with her dog, just like every other morning before work.

After snapping photos of the man's hands, she leaned in for a closer look. One hand was covered in blood, but the other clutched a few fibers. As a hairdresser, Sassy knew it was hair. In the early morning light, she could only tell the hair had been processed. The very blond, almost white, color wasn't natural.

She took a few more photos, stood, and walked back toward Bracken, whose tail wagged so furiously, she actually scattered the stones behind her.

Something flashed past, startling her. She spun to see where the object landed. Watching where she stepped, she carefully made her way over to see what it was.

"A ring!"

An engagement ring by the style of it—a narrow, gold band with a small diamond. If it was an engagement ring, it was very modest in its simple design and small stone. Her heart ached for the woman who had lost it, or the man who had yet to present it to the love of his life.

She gazed back at the man again. Was it connected to this man or had someone else lost it and it was just a coincidence it was here now?

She snapped a few pictures of the ring then stacked several rocks on top of each other as a marker for when the Guards finally arrived.

Chapter Three

She had never been so happy to be home as she was in that moment.

After she'd been allowed to leave the scene, she and Bracken had run along the main road which got them home quicker. Their normal morning routine was to run the two miles from Bettystown up the beach to the river. Make the mile loop around the houses along the small peninsula at Mornington, then run back via the beach for home. Five miles total. The wolfhound loved the exercise, and it helped get some blood into her own system before having to stand all day working on hair.

When she'd been looking for salon space, she was lucky to find a small two-story cottage overlooking the strand right in the center of Bettystown village. The place was being sold as potential commercial space, which was ideal for her needs. She had everything she wanted on her doorstep, and if she needed anything else, her old Mini was parked in the little garage out back. The only thing that made her happier was she had qualified for the mortgage.

She'd still had work to do on the place. The salon had to be fitted out, and the upstairs needed to be converted into a two-bedroom flat, with a kitchen and all mod-cons. At the same time, she built an exterior entrance to the flat at the back.

What could be better?

She and Bracken dashed up those back stairs, and as soon as they were through the door, Bracken rushed to her bowl and gulped the water down like she'd been starved, then found her bed.

As Sassy rushed to get her shower, she couldn't blame the dog for her thirst. The Guards had kept them at the scene a lot longer than she had expected. Other than her own tea and the slice of toast she'd shared with Bracken, neither had eaten before their run, and the Guards hadn't even offered a lift home. By the time they arrived, they were both parched.

Sassy found Bracken in the same place fifteen minutes later, after showering and dressing for work. She gave the dog a handful of dog biscuits and a cuddle before checking her hair in the small mirror by the door before leaving for work.

She ran her fingers through the short bob she normally wore which framed her petite face. Even to her own brown eyes, the cut highlighted her high cheekbones. Her naturally dark hair was dyed a shimmery red, though she saw the dark roots starting to appear. Mary could soon sort that out, but it wouldn't be today.

Even though Sassy lived upstairs, she was still very late, but as the owner of Sassy Cuts, she didn't feel obliged to explain herself.

As she opened the interior door into the salon, that expectation was quashed. Her ten o'clock appointment sat in the waiting area with an expression on her face that could freeze water in Hell. Sassy didn't have to look at the clock to know it was going on noon. Yes, Mrs. Ellison would have to be the appointment she'd stood up, wouldn't she?

She rushed over to the woman to offer the explanation that only moments ago she had said she didn't have to give.

"Mrs. Ellison, I'm so—"

"Miss O'Brien," the woman cut in, standing and gathering her things off the sofa beside her. The woman's demeanor and inflection always reminded her of Mrs. Slocum minus the colored hair from *Are You Being Served?*—a bit above herself and a little condescending, but in a charming sort of way that actually made her an interesting woman.

Mrs. Ellison was an older English woman who had relocated to Ireland, but why she chose such a small village like Bettystown, Sassy would never know. The woman only ever talked about her life in England, when she did converse at all during her appointments.

"If you were going to leave me left waiting for my appointment, it would have been the courteous thing to do to ring." She rolled the R.

After two hours, Sassy wondered why the woman was still here at all. "I really am very sorry, Mrs. Ellison. It couldn't be helped." Sassy motioned toward her workstation. "I'm here now and we can get started."

The old woman waved her away. "I haven't the time now." She pushed past Sassy and headed for the door.

"Shall we reschedule your appointment before you leave? I'll give you a discount for the inconvenience." Sassy moved behind the reception desk to where the appointment book lay open.

"I don't think so." And the woman was gone.

"Well . . ." What else could she say? She could hardly blame the woman for being angry. There had just been no way for her to ring while being repeatedly interrogated, from the Guards to the inspectors.

She shook her head, trying to clear her thoughts, and consulted her appointment book. Mrs. Fitzgerald, noon. Just as well to not rush now that she didn't have to.

Sassy gazed at the clock and headed for the little kitchen at the back. She had five minutes for a cuppa, and to calm down.

"You've never been this late before," Mary said, entering the kitchen as Sassy switched on the kettle.

She pulled her mug from the shelf and dropped a tea bag into it, then held her palm up to the woman and said, "Please, God, I never will be again." She didn't really want to talk about what had happened this morning. At the same time, she was bursting at the seams to tell *someone*. How could she let something as monumental as finding a dead body go without mention? It's not like it happened every day.

"Are you all right, Sass? Your hands are shaking. I know you can handle Mrs. Ellison. She'll be back once she calms down." Mary pulled the biscuits from the cupboard and set out a second cup.

"I know. I can't believe I totally forgot about her." That was a half truth. Once she realized the time, she remembered the appointment, but couldn't make the call.

"That's unlike you. What happened?"

Sassy knew her friend would get it out of her eventually.

She glanced down the short hall into to the salon to be sure her appointment hadn't arrived yet. The only other person in the salon was a woman under a blow dryer. She wouldn't hear anything.

Sassy pulled her mobile out of her back pocket, opened the gallery app, and thrust the phone in Mary's direction. It was a split second before her hand flew to her open mouth. The woman's eyes bulged as she took in what was on the screen.

Sassy scrolled to a few other images before putting the phone back in her pocket.

"What the hell, Sassy?" Incredulity poured from her friend's voice.

"I know, right? And keep your voice down."

The kettle clicked off and Sassy poured steaming water into both cups. Just as she reached for a biscuit she didn't think she could stomach, Mary started laughing. "Oh! You got me. Good one." She grabbed her cup and headed back toward the salon.

Sassy grabbed her by the arm, stopping her at the door. "This isn't a joke, Mary," she said under her breath. "I was running Bracken on the beach this morning, like I always do, and . . . there he was." She thrust her hand toward the floor, as if the body was still in front of her. In her mind's eye, he still was. She didn't think she would ever get rid of the image of him lying there, his blood drained out of him, his pale face and grey lips.

She started shaking again.

"Oh my God." Mary hugged her quickly, then looked into her eyes. "Do you know what happened?"

She gave her friend a quick rundown of the morning. Mrs. Fitzgerald walked through the door just as Sassy finished her story. "Are you fit enough to work on yer wan?" Mary asked, nodding to the waiting customer.

"I think so."

"You should take the day off. I'll sort her out for you."

"No, I need the distraction. If I leave, Bracken will just want back on the beach and frankly, I don't think I could handle it. They're probably still down there anyway. I don't need to be hovering, do I? I need this." She patted Mary's hand and grabbed her cup of tea.

"Go the other direction. The Guards aren't in Laytown now. They're all in Mornington at the investigation."

"No. Thanks. I'll be okay. Really. It was just a shock, is all. I'll be all right once I get back in the rhythm."

"Well, if you change your mind, let me know. I have a slow schedule this afternoon."

"Thanks, you're very good."

Chapter Four

Sassy was checking the appointment book on the counter when she heard the salon door open. She'd just waved goodbye to Mrs. Fitzgerald, and while the salon was empty just then, she saw there were two more clients today before she could go home. She just hoped it wasn't Mrs. Ellison, back to give Sassy another piece of her mind for standing her up.

It wasn't, nor was it her next appointment. The last person she expected to see was a smartly dressed man entering her establishment. Given the familiar face, he could only want one thing.

"Detective Donnelly." Tossing down her pen, she stuck her hands out, wrists together, and gave him a look that said, "We are not amused." His interrogation this morning hadn't gone well, so she was sure this wasn't going to be pleasant either. She hadn't mentioned her own sleuthing. Had he found out she had taken photos and now wanted them?

"What's that for when it's at home?" he asked, flicking his gaze to her outstretched wrists.

"You've come to arrest me, right? Why else would you be here? You haven't found any clues and no one has stepped forward saying they did it. I'm the only witness . . . and I'm guessing your only suspect. So arrest me and let's get this over with. I've got a dog waiting to go out."

"You mean that pony?"

She gave him an annoyed smirk and pushed her wrists toward him.

"Put those away. I'm not arresting you. Unless you're into handcuffs . . . " He gave her a cheeky wink.

A snicker came from behind her. Sassy knew without looking Mary had appeared from the kitchen and now focused on the situation.

To be honest, Detective Donnelly wasn't hard on the eyes. He met all the traditional requirements of an officer of *An Garda Síochána*—he was over six feet in height, broad shouldered, had neatly trimmed hair, and a very stern expression. While it was a different story for inspectors who could carry a weapon, Irish Guards needed an impressive build and stern looks since they weren't allowed to carry firearms. Right now though, the only look he was giving her was anything but stern, and his build certainly was impressive.

He also met her requirements as a man. As a stylist, she was sure his dark hair would curl if he let it grow out. She loved men with curly hair. His soft, green eyes were almost hypnotic when he gazed at her, even while he took her statement when he'd arrived on the scene earlier in the day. He wasn't all muscly like the cops she saw on American crime programs, but he was athletically built; he took care of himself.

And there was that . . . something . . . he emitted when he stood close. She thought about the handcuffs, but shook off the feeling as she tried concentrating on why he was in her shop—not that she wouldn't mind being handcuffed by this sexy Guard, mind you. She wasn't sure whether to laugh with him or be horrified he was making light of a serious situation.

"Are you saying I'm not a suspect?" she asked, defensively crossing her arms in front of her and pulling her thoughts back in the right direction.

"No, you're a suspect, all right. Just not a serious one."

"Then what are you doing here? I told you everything."

"Sometimes people later remember things . . . once they've had a chance to relax from the shock."

"I'm pretty sure I remember everything. You kept me waiting long enough after I rang. I had plenty of time to think about things. It's not like I finished my jog then came back when I saw the squad car pulling up."

In reality, an officer had arrived on the scene less than fifteen minutes after her call to 999. It had just felt like she'd waited half the day.

Village Garda stations kept regular business hours, like the bank, rather than having someone there round the clock like the stations in town. While a local officer had been called into work early to meet her at the scene, the investigators had to make the drive from the district headquarters in Ashbourne, forty-five minutes away.

"To be fair, you did ring us before our morning coffee and donuts. It was fierce early."

He made the statement so seriously, it took her a moment to realize he was teasing her again. Not missing a beat, she flicked her gaze to his tight midsection.

"It's a good thing no one sells proper donuts in Ireland or you and that six-pack would soon part company."

He chuckled again. "Right you are."

"Sassy makes great donuts."

Both Sassy and Detective Donnelly shot glances over at Mary and found her hovering closer than she'd been a moment before.

"Do you, now?" Donnelly asked.

Giving Mary a *shut up and go'way* look, Sassy said, "They're not donuts. They're beignets. They're out of a box I bought in New Orleans last year when I was on holiday." She turned back to the Guard when the woman left to tidy her workstation.

One of his eyebrows arched, and his mouth lifted on one side with a smirk.

"What?"

"I like beignets."

"You would." Taking a deep breath, she asked, "So, what

17

do you think I know that I haven't told you . . . because of my frazzled state?" She put her hands up and waved them about, shaking her head and made a face like she was crazy.

With a snicker, Donnelly pulled out his notepad. He flipped through the pages, backtracked, then flipped through again. Finally, he found the page he wanted. Looking up he said, "With all the excitement, I didn't get your number."

She didn't have to think about it. "Yesyoudid" came out as a single word. "It was one of the first things you asked me—name, address, and phone number. I even gave you my business card. See?" She reached over and pulled her card from the back of the notepad where she was pretty sure he'd hidden it. And not very well.

A rosy blush shot across the man's cheeks. "Caught me." He leaned in and lowered his voice. "I was hoping for your personal number."

"Isn't that a bit unprofessional? I mean, I am a suspect, however serious."

"I know you didn't do it, and it won't take long for the investigators to know you didn't do it either. Besides, I'm a man of action, so why wait when we both know the outcome?"

Man of action? Cheeky git more likely.

Sexy as he was . . . tempted as *she* was . . . she wasn't interested. Especially not under these circumstances.

"Sorry, I'm seeing someone."

"No, you're not." Mary was stealth if nothing else. Sassy didn't have to turn around to tell how close the woman was again. The nearness of her voice gave away her location.

Without acknowledging her, Sassy gave a tight smile and said, "We just broke up."

"Six months ago."

Sassy pressed her lips together and squeezed her eyes shut so tightly she saw stars. Her friend meant well. Mary had been trying to set her up for weeks now. Said her attitude needed some adjusting and knew a bloke with the right tool.

As much as Sassy loved her friend, would the woman ever just shut up?

When she opened her eyes again, Detective Donnelly was still there. Grinning at her.

"If I tell you something I left out earlier, will you please leave my shop?" She prayed he'd say yes.

The stern Garda look crossed his face just then. It almost scared her. "Withholding evidence?"

"It's not like your crack forensics team won't eventually discover it anyway."

He didn't say anything but continued staring at her, his notebook at the ready.

"Do you promise not to arrest me?"

"No."

She rolled her eyes and recrossed her arms in frustration. "Figures." She took a deep breath. "Okay, while I was sitting waiting for you to finish your donuts, I noticed something in the man's hand."

Ignoring her comment, he said, "Yes, unknown fibers. They're on their way for analysis now."

"Well, I can tell you it's human hair."

"How do you know that?"

Sassy lifted an eyebrow and flicked her gaze into the salon's interior.

"Hairdresser. Gotcha." He made notes on the pad. "Is there anything else?"

"Yeah, it wasn't the hair's natural color. It had been processed. Platinum, I believe."

"And what color is that . . . some kind of yellow?"

"No, almost white." She dug out a box of sample hair extensions from under the counter and withdrew the one she thought most closely matched the color of the hair in the dead man's hands. "These are made from real hair. I'm almost positive this is the same color as what the man had in his hand. It was hard to tell since there were so few strands, but I'm pretty sure. No, I'm very sure."

Donnelly took the hair sample in his hand and looked at it. "Can I take this with me?"

"Why? This is my sample box."

"Just to rule out—"

"I get it." She put up her hand to stop him. "To rule out that I didn't plant the hairs on the victim. In that case, have at it." She pulled a small paper sack from beside the register that was emblazoned with Sassy Cuts across one side in big, bold purple letters, and slipped the sample extension into it. "Here's your evidence bag."

Donnelly chuckled at her. "Thanks. Are you some super sleuth in your spare time or something?"

Sassy froze. She thought her heart was going to fall out though her kneecaps, it had plummeted so hard. Had he found out she'd been snooping around the body?

"Umm, no, why?" She fidgeted with items on the desk, hoping to block out his intrusion as she tidied.

He stuffed the sack with the hair extension it in into his jacket and said, "You have the lingo down."

"What do you mean?"

"Well, at the beach you called the man a victim when I took your statement and did again just now. You obviously looked around while you waited because you pointed out the ring. And thanks for leaving it *in situ* until we got here. Much appreciated. Now you're all about evidence bags and expecting to be arrested because you're our only witness. What gives?"

She hid her fear with an unnatural laugh. "Oh, that. I watch a lot of crime drama."

Apparently she'd piqued his interest. "Really? There are some good programs on at the moment. What do you like?"

She shook her head. "I don't know. The usual I guess . . . Bones, CSI . . . Castle."

He just nodded as she spoke. "I liked The Wire. Too bad it's over now."

"Too gritty for me. Though I do like Criminal Minds."

Donnelly noticeably cringed. "And that show isn't gritty? That one messes with your head."

She laughed. "Ye big girl's blouse."

That snapped him to attention. "So, is that it? No other secrets you want to share?" He stuffed the notebook into another pocket.

"About the crime scene? No. If you don't need anything else from me, I can see my next appointment on her way in."

"I guess I'm not getting your personal number then."

"'Fraid not."

"What if I have more questions?" He did look hopeful.

Sassy fanned out her arms around the salon. "You know where to find me."

Chapter Five

Over the next several days, murder on the beach was on everyone's lips. Locals asked the same questions Sassy had also asked—Who was he? What happened? Who did it? And more.

Mary had kept her promise. They'd had a long talk, and Sassy was satisfied her friend wouldn't tell anyone about what happened that morning. She wished it had never happened, and appreciated Mary's confidence.

Murder in this region was so rare it quickly became village gossip. Sassy was most appreciative that Detective Donnelly had kept her name out of the press as the one who discovered the body. Otherwise, her salon would have been flooded with local busybodies and, no doubt, the media too, all wanting to know what she saw. Not only did she not have time for any of it, she prided herself on not being a gossip, in spite of her career choice which was notorious for it.

Plus, she valued her privacy. She appreciated her quiet life outside the salon. The minute someone figured out she was involved, however minutely, she'd never hear the end of it.

Worse, every morning when she woke, she was sure Donnelly, or one of the other guards, would be knocking on her door with an arrest warrant for tampering with the body. She knew she had nothing to be afraid of, but it still niggled her.

She was deep in thought when her client, Mrs. Kennedy, said, "Sassy, I didn't know you cut men's hair. I should bring himself in for a trim."

Sassy looked up and saw Detective Donnelly standing at the reception desk. Had his ears been burning when she was thinking about him just now?

"I don't, Mrs. Kennedy. I'll just see what he wants. Won't be a moment."

She approached Donnelly with the casual smile on her face she reserved for customers so that her salon full of women didn't become suspicious.

"Miss O'Brien—" he started but she cut him off.

"If you're looking for the barber, he's just around the corner. Let me show you." She grasped him by the elbow and walked him out the door. She pointed up the street, as if giving him directions. "Please, you can't come into my place of business like this. They can't know I was involved. You promised."

She followed Donnelly's glance through the salon window. All eyes were turned their direction. He smiled with a look of understanding.

"I'm sorry. You're right. What I'm doing now is pretending like I'm confused and we'll walk this way, as if you're taking me to the barber. Just nod."

She did as he asked and led him out of sight of her nosy customers. She was grateful her salon was just off the village square so the people going about their business wouldn't overhear either.

"Thank you," she said sincerely. "Now, what's this about?"

He pulled some paper out of his pocket and unfolded it. "This is the report that came back on the hair. You were right. It belonged to a woman, and was dyed platinum."

Sassy couldn't help but grin. She did know her hair. "Thanks for telling me. It's nice to see I'm not losing my touch." She started walking away but halted at his words.

"You might want to hear the rest of this. You're not going to like it."

She didn't want to look at him but slowly turned back. What now? She had nothing to do with this. "Isn't this the part you say, You might want to sit down for this?"

"I would, but you've already told me you don't want to go out with me."

"What does this have to do with going out with you?"

He motioned across the road. "I could take you across to the café for a coffee and tell you what I have to say, but you might take it as a date."

She rolled her eyes at him.

When he didn't say anything more, she gazed into his green eyes for a long moment. Just then, she didn't see the Garda detective or the cheeky git who'd tried getting her number from her in the salon a few days earlier. She thought she saw sincerity in his all-too-handsome face.

She stood before him with her hands in the pockets of her work apron. Crossing her arms in front of herself would have been defensive, and she didn't want to be. "I never said I wouldn't go out with you. You never asked."

"I asked for your number," he reminded her.

"Not the same."

"How else was I going to ask you out?"

She pointed her thumb over her shoulder and said, "You've been to the salon twice now. It's not like you don't know where to find me." She softly smiled at him.

His lips curved up on one edge and his cheeks filled with a rosy flush, which she found kind of cute. He was a pleasant change from men who were usually too full of themselves for their own good. Sure, as a Garda detective, he would have to be tough and all business, but he'd let down his guard just enough to show her he wasn't always like that.

"You're a better detective than I am."

"I doubt it." She was sure the ladies were wondering where she was, but she didn't care. Sassy found she was actually enjoying Donnelly's company. He was fun to tease. But, he did say he had some news she might not want to hear. After a short silence, she asked, "Are you going to tell me about this news I really should be sitting down for?"

He glanced back at the evidence report. "We were able to figure out the manufacturer on that hair dye."

"Really? That's great. You guys have some amazing equipment to be able to do that. Why wouldn't I like this information? By the way, should you even be sharing this stuff with me? I mean, especially as I'm a suspect in an ongoing investigation and everything."

"I thought you should hear it from me rather than someone else."

"Well then, spit it out. You've got me in suspenders." She winked, hoping to keep this light.

He pointed to the report and showed her the result. The maker of the dye is called Starlet. The shade is Platinum Bombshell. "You recognize this?"

"Of course. We're the only authorized seller in Leinster."

"We know that too."

"What does this mean?"

"It means one of two things. One, either you did plant the evidence, or two, whoever did had their hair done in your shop."

Sassy wasn't sure what to say after that. She swayed on her feet a little and Donnelly's reached out a hand to steady her by her arm. "I'm okay. Thanks." Instinctively, she put her hand on his for reassurance. The warmth of it seemed to help her digest what he'd just told her.

"Keep in mind, I still don't think you had anything to do with this.".

She tried chuckling but it came out more like a huff. "Thanks for that. I know I didn't have anything to do with it. I've been going crazy trying to figure out why I had to be the one who found him. Hundreds of people walk that beach every day. Why me?" She gazed into his eyes, hoping for an answer. All she saw was empathy, which would have to do. "Do I need to worry?"

"No, but do you have a client list of everyone who uses this product? If so, do I need to get a warrant for this information?"

"Absolutely not. I'll cooperate any way I can. I'll speak with Mary and have a list for you by tomorrow. Is that all right . . . is that soon enough?" She hoped it was because right now her brain was so frazzled she couldn't think of one person who came in for platinum blonde hair.

She gazed along the main street of the village from where they stood, hoping to spot just one woman with platinum hair, but everyone at that very moment seemed dark haired.

"Tomorrow will be fine. Hey."

When he put the backs of his fingers on her cheek, she realized she still held his hand on her arm.

"You look a little pale. You going to be all right?"

Was he really so comfortable to be with? It was only the third time she'd talked with him, and already he seemed to be weaseling his way into her senses.

She nodded quickly. "Just when I thought I was convincing you I had no part in this, I find it's all staring me right in the face. I'm a little shocked, is all. I'll be all right." Glancing back toward the salon, she remembered her client was still in the chair. "I need to get back inside. Thanks, I think, for letting me know. See you tomorrow." Glancing over her shoulder on her way back to the salon, she added, "Come around noon. You can buy me that coffee."

His laughter followed her as she entered the salon.

Chapter Six

A narrow road leading onto the beach was all that separated Sassy's from Chutney Café, where she was meeting Detective Donnelly. A portion of the beach was reserved for overflow car parking for the village's small amusement park. It was where local hobby fisherman accessed the sea to launch their skiffs. And it was the starting point for her morning runs with Bracken.

Today she had missed her run in order to get her salon chores done so she would be free to meet Donnelly at noon, but she was still breathless when she stepped through the door and watched his long frame rise from his seat near a sea view window. Clutching the paperwork he'd requested in her hand, she took a deep breath to calm her nerves and moved toward him.

"Thanks for meeting me." He pulled out a chair for her across from his.

She didn't bother removing her coat because she wasn't planning on staying long. But before she could stop him, he ordered Americanos for two from the waitress, Fiona, who had followed her to the table.

"How did you know I prefer coffee over tea?" She set the documents aside and settled back in her seat, watching as he pulled his long legs under the table.

"Yesterday, when you said I could buy you coffee. I figured you preferred it over tea or you would have said I could buy you tea."

She couldn't help but laugh. "Which is why you're the

27

detective, and I just cut hair."

His grin reached his eyes when he said, "Based on our evidence, I doubt you 'just cut hair.' I'd say you're quite the expert." He paused. "Maybe one day you'll cut my hair."

She narrowed her gaze at him. Not because she wasn't interested in cutting his hair, but at the thought of getting her fingers into the curls she was sure he was suppressing with his tight detective's cut.

"I don't normally cut men's hair, but I might make one exception."

Fiona quickly returned with their coffees. Sassy didn't miss the woman's gaze at Donnelly, scowling before returning behind the counter to fill another order.

Sassy ignored the woman as she and Donnelly settled into a comfortable silence as they prepared their coffees—a drop of milk for him and a good lashing for her, and a spoon of sugar. Her spoon clinked on the inside edges of the cup as she nervously stirred.

What did she have to be nervous about? It wasn't like detectives wore the traditional Garda uniform. For all Fiona knew, Sassy was meeting a friend for coffee and not with a detective from *An Garda Síochána*. Typical of Irish villages though, many knew it had been a while since she'd dated, so seeing her with a man—a very good looking man—was bound to wag a few chins.

She wished it hadn't been Fiona working today. She didn't need the drama. Especially from her. Sassy had promised herself no more drama when she kicked Seamus to the curb. His sister would eventually learn their break up was none of her business.

What Sassy needed now though, was to get this over. She'd give Donnelly the documents, finish her coffee, and then go back to work.

Great. She had a plan.

"So." She handed him the documents. "I brought what you asked for." She was surprised when he set them aside.

28

"Aren't you going to look at it?"

"When I get back into the office where I won't be distracted."

"Oh, well then—"

As she moved to push back her chair to leave, his hand was on her arm. "Sit. Finish your coffee. You just got here."

Sassy sat back in her chair and regained her comfortable-uncomfortable state. She was actually starting to enjoy his company, but also found the whole situation disconcerting. She was a suspect with at least one clue pointing in her direction. She knew it was a coincidence, and Donnelly had told her she was only a minor suspect, and that he was sure she didn't have anything to do with the man's demise. But at the same time, what if someone was framing her for some reason? She shivered at the thought.

"You all right?"

"Yeah, why?" She sipped her coffee. The heat of it traced a path to her belly. Or was that Donnelly's gaze doing that to her?

"You shivered and pulled your jacket more firmly around yourself."

She hadn't noticed. "I'm just anxious about the evidence leading to my shop. Someone on that list may have had something to do with that poor man's death," she said in a low voice, looking around to be sure no one was eavesdropping on their conversation. Especially Fiona. "One of my clients could be a murderer. Or would that be a murderess?" She nervously sipped her coffee again.

His palm covered her hand this time. Something else warm worked its way through her just then.

"We'll get to the bottom of it." He gazed at her for a long moment before reaching for the documents. "If it makes you feel better, let's look at what you brought." He flipped through the pages. "There are more names here than I expected."

"As I said yesterday, I have exclusive rights in the region to sell this product. People come from all over the province for it. I even have clients from the North who come down for this particular shade."

The current trend was not just traditional platinum, but a shade hinting at white. It was all the rage since Game of Thrones began airing on telly. Suddenly, women wanted the hair of Daenerys Targaryen.

That's what made the fibers in the man's hand stand out for her. Naturally greying hair was obvious, often including strands with both the natural color and grey as colors changed along the shaft. She'd even seen strands of hair that reminded her of zebra strips, where the natural dark color and grey changed more than once along a single shaft. The fibers on the victim were of consistent coloring which had told her the hair was most definitely dyed.

He looked deep in thought, then suggested, "Bettystown is still a resort of sorts. It's possible the suspect came from outside the region."

She hadn't thought of that. "Possibly but I don't remember any strangers coming in for treatment. Do you want me to ring the other shops that stock this brand for their client lists?"

Donnelly looked contemplative for a moment. "Let's see where your list gets us first. If all of these women check out, we'll look outside of Leinster."

To her surprise, Donnelly shifted his chair around to sit beside her rather than work across the table. He pulled the documents with him and opened them in the space between their cups. He pulled out a pen from a pocket inside his jacket. "Let's go through this list. Give me as much information on each person as possible that you think can help us narrow the list to real suspects."

She nodded and they got to work. Oddly, she was grateful he let her help. In a way, it proved to her that he didn't think of her as a suspect. Not really a partner either, but at least he was keeping her in the loop. In a way, it satisfied her curiosity about crime scene investigation. Beckett would be proud!

An hour and another Americano later, they'd whittled down the list to a handful of suspects. They'd crossed out older women who wouldn't have the strength or wherewithal for such a crime. As well, they removed clients who hadn't been in for a very long time, and those clients who'd changed shades before the murder.

This left them with a shortlist of young to middle-aged women. Still more than she would have liked. Sassy just wanted this over so she could get on with her life, such as it was for a single woman who buried herself in work so she didn't have to think about being single.

Chapter Seven

Bracken hated her. The poor wolfhound's forlorn look filled the rearview mirror. She couldn't blame the dog. She barely fit into the backseat of the old Mini. It was only a half hour drive to Clogherhead though, then the dog could run and stretch her legs. And hopefully forgive her mistress for stuffing her into the little car.

Sassy needed a break from all the drama in Bettystown. She wished more than ever that she hadn't been the one to find the body. She wished the hair in the victim's hand wasn't the rare shade only she stocked in all of Ireland, which she confirmed yesterday by ringing the other three salons around the country that stocked Starlet products.

And she wished she could stop thinking about Donnelly, full stop. He was too sexy for his, or her, own good. She was pretty sure he knew it too.

Focusing on the road, she carefully drove through Clogherhead Village, passing rows and rows of traditional cottages that had seen better days, some still occupied and others not. New homes dotted the roadside on the way into the village. And more than one estate full of cookie-cutter homes had been built during the Celtic Tiger years, some of which were halted mid-construction when the banks stopped lending money.

She passed through the village, turned onto Harbour Road, and headed for Port Oriel. The drive took her over a gently rolling hillside, though the Mini's suspension gave no clue to the smooth, newly laid road. It seemed every pebble and imperfection in the tarmac was a major obstacle for the little car. Bracken whined more than once as they bumped along.

"Sorry, Bracken. We're nearly there."

As they came over the last rise before the port, the Irish Sea opened before them. Low clouds had lifted to reveal the Mourne Mountains of County Down, some twenty miles away as the crow flies. The impressive mountains were visible right down the coast as far as Skerries. Another reason she enjoyed running along the strand from Bettystown to Mornington—the mountains and their ever changing personality.

As soon as Bracken caught the scent of salty air, her whines changed from woe-is-me to I-know-where-we-are-hurry-up-for-the-love-of-god-I-know-where-we-are-let-me-out-before-I-burst!

Sassy couldn't help but grin. She was happy to be here too. Especially because of the man they came to visit for the weekend.

She'd barely pulled into a parking space overlooking the quay where the ships were moored when there was a sharp knock on the passenger window. A rough hand pulled open the door and freed the dog.

"You need a bigger car if you're going to keep bringing your pony with you." The dog bounded in circles around him, her forlorn look now replaced with one of pure, unadulterated joy. He dodged and chased Bracken around the car as if they were two children playing tag.

Sassy grinned at the two as she locked the passenger door from the inside and then got out of the car and locked the driver's door. "You're going to need a bigger house, Liam, if you want us to keep visiting you. That chicken coop you live in is barely big enough for one person, let alone guests."

"Since when have you ever been a guest. Pest more likely."

Sassy rounded the car and threw her arms around her brother. A boatman, he was solid muscle and easily lifted her off her feet in a big hug. She needed this—the familiarity, the relaxation . . . the comfort. She squeezed him tightly.

"It's great to see you, Sass. It's been a while since you were up."

"I know," she said, back on her feet and leaning down to open the tiny boot where her overnight bag and Bracken's gear were stowed. "I've been really busy."

"Business good or is that just an excuse?" His wink when she looked up told her he knew she'd never make excuses for not coming up to see him. Ever since they were kids, she'd loved his teasing and banter.

"Business is really good. But like you said, it's been too long, and since you can't seem to ever make it to Bettystown, I guess the duty falls on me to come up here if I want to see your sorry self." It was her turn to wink. She could dish it out as well as he could. That was just one of the things she loved about Liam. Their visits were always lighthearted and relaxing.

She desperately needed relaxing.

Liam huffed as he grabbed Bracken's gear. "You can carry your own bag. It's heavier than this one. I know how you pack."

"Lazy," she called after him as he headed up the short path leading to a small cottage at the crest of the hill that overlooked the harbor. "I guess I'll carry these homemade biscuits as well. I hope I don't drop them with my heavy bag and all."

Liam was back down the path in a blink. He grabbed up her bag and slung it over his shoulder, carried Bracken's bag in one hand, and grabbed the plastic container full of biscuits in the other. He was back on the path and trotting beside the dog who bounced along excitedly.

Sassy laughed. She knew how to play her brother, all right.

That evening, the three huddled in a snug at the Oriel Pub. Being in such a remote area, the publican turned a blind eye to dogs as long as they minded themselves. After what Bracken probably perceived as the drive from hell, she was lying quietly at their feet, mostly under the table.

Their meals done and the table cleared, they settled in for a pint or two before the short stroll home.

"You're very quiet."

She sighed. "Long week. I'm glad it's over."

"I hear they found a body on the beach. I'd say the village is hopping with gossip." Liam took a long swallow from the black ale in front of him.

He would have to bring up the one thing she was trying to escape. "Yes, too much gossip for my liking. I wish people would mind their own business." Even she heard the irritation in her voice.

"You all right?" Even though she'd just snapped, Liam's voice was calm. He was genuinely concerned.

"Sorry for snapping. Yes, things are fine. Just tired. The whole . . . issue . . . has been very draining. I just wanted to be somewhere quiet for a while. At the moment, Bettystown is anything but quiet."

Liam chuckled. "So you came to me for quiet? Good luck with that."

"I don't know what I was thinking." She rolled her eyes dramatically for his benefit.

Taking a sip of her shandy, she tried pulling herself into the shadows of the snug. The long week, the bumpy drive, and a full belly made her want to just lie back and sleep the weekend out. Liam wouldn't allow it though. She was sure he had something planned for them to do.

Thankfully, he let the subject of the murder drop. She closed her eyes as she listened to the background music filtering through the pub, broken by snippets of conversation and laughter, clinking of glasses behind the bar, and Donnelly's voice filling her senses.

She wished she could get him out of her mind, but there was something about him. He was a bit of a flirt, but a lot of Irishmen were. It meant nothing. Usually what came out of their mouths didn't meet their eyes. With Donnelly, it seemed he spoke to her through his gaze. That unnerved her.

His mention of handcuffs, his gentle touch on her cheek, the warmth of his palm covering her hand, the suggestion she cut his hair . . . They all seemed like invitations to her. Her heart beat a little faster at the thought of it all, and more.

"Let's get you home."

Her brother's voice forced itself into her head. "Mmm, what?" She opened one eye and saw Liam grinning at her, and not Donnelly. She was almost disappointed.

"I said, let's get you home. If you're falling asleep in the pub, you must be tired."

Sassy looked at her watch. Had she really dozed? "Oh my God, Liam, I'm so sorry. I'm awake now. Let's have another drink. We have some catching up to do."

He slid from the snug, making sure not to step on Bracken. "We've got all day tomorrow. We'll make it an easy day. A couple of cans, a little fishing, and what do you girls call it? Oh, yes. A chinwag."

She snickered as she extricated herself from her all too comfortable seat. "A chinwag, eh? I'd like that. Come on, then." She snapped the lead on Bracken and the three headed out into the night for the short stroll home.

Chapter Eight

It was a good thing they headed home early last night because Liam got them up at the crack of dawn to go fishing. He hadn't been teasing about that. It had been a long time since they'd fished together. They used to do it when they were children. It was one of her fondest memories of growing up with him. There had only been the pair of them in the family, with other kids to play with a long walk away. They'd grown up in each other's hip pocket and developed a strong bond.

Liam had loved the sea since he was old enough to know what it was; he'd always talked about boats and often took her to the dock to watch the ships come in. It was no wonder he became a boatman.

Port Oriel was a quiet but active harbor. Fishing vessels that used the port as their home base were often out at sea for a week or two at a time. She'd picked the perfect time to visit Liam. She wanted quiet and it seemed like most ships were out working at the moment.

Sassy watched Bracken sniffing along the edge of the grass where it met the rugged coastline. It had been a short walk from the cottage to their fishing spot—out the backdoor, across the rough grass just barely clinging to the headland, and there they were. She saw the roof on the cottage from where she sat; they were that close.

She closed her eyes for a moment and savored the silence. Though it really wasn't quiet. Gentle, tidal waves lapped the rocks, the sea breeze blew against them and flapped their clothing, and the occasional sea bird squawked as it wheeled in the air. When the breeze picked up, an old, brass bell clanged on one of the boats still docked on the quay, rocking with the movement in the water. She inhaled deeply of the sea air, appreciating all the sounds that made up her peaceful calm.

"You're not falling asleep again, are you? Some houseguest you're turning out to be."

"I'm not falling asleep," she assured him. "I'm just appreciating the peacefulness. I really needed this. Thanks."

Just then she felt a tug on her line and, as always, Liam was right by her side to coach her into hauling in her catch. They'd always had some sort of friendly bet. Today, it was whoever caught the first fish got to relax while the other did the cooking for dinner.

"Looks like you're cooking, *buachaill*." She flashed him a smug grin and started reeling in her fish.

A moment later, the tip of Liam's line jerked and he rushed over to where the rod was wedged upright in the rocks. "Oh, no, not if I get mine in first."

She was not going to let his size, strength, and experience win. She pulled up on the rod, then spun the reel as the rod relaxed. She pulled up again and repeated until she was sure the fish would soon be landed.

Chancing a glance, she looked at her brother to see him doing the same thing, though he seemed to be giving it more effort than she. Did that mean that not only would he land the first fish and she'd be cooking—a fine thing to be doing when she was meant to be relaxing on her short holiday—but his fish would also be bigger? The way her week was going, this fit right in.

Suddenly, Liam's body jerked and he nearly lost his footing. The line snapped, and whatever had been on the other end was making its getaway.

With one more pull on the rod, Sassy's fish popped out of the water to dangle and flap at the end of the line.

That is, if it could be called a fish. Fish bait more likely, by the size of it. Oh, well. She gently unhooked the tiny fish and released it back into the water.

"Looks like we'll go hungry tonight at this rate," she said.

Liam came to sit beside her. He opened the little cooler he'd brought with them and handed her half a sandwich and a can of lager. "You do remember I'm your brother, right? The last thing you have to worry about is going hungry with me."

Sassy laughed. "True." She took a bite of the plain white bread sandwich which he'd lashed with real butter and a slice of ham. She hadn't had an old-fashioned sandwich like this in donkey's years, and right now, it was the best-tasting sandwich she'd had in a very long time. Quite possibly because she was having it here and now, and not really for what it was.

Liam took a long swallow of his beer, washing down the last of a second half of his sandwich, let out a mighty belch, and grinned.

She laughed again. "Men!"

"Sue me." He gazed out to sea for a moment. Was he reveling in the peace here, or wishing he was out there on the water? Before she could ask, he turned to gaze at her. "You going to tell me what's going on?"

She felt her back stiffen. "Nothing's going on."

"Sure it is. I mentioned the murder last night, and you shut me out. You looked tired, so I let it go. But you've been very quiet since you got here, so I know something has you rattled."

His gaze bored into her. She didn't really want to talk about it, but at the same time, he'd be the calm head of reason she needed right now.

She pulled out her mobile phone, opened the photo gallery, and pulled up the start of the photos she'd taken that morning on the river's edge.

Handing the device over, Liam took it and used a rough finger to swipe the screen. His gaze narrowed, and his features darkened with each swipe. When he was done, he back-scrolled the images to take a second look. Handing her back the phone, he asked, "What's your involvement in this?"

There was no way to sugarcoat it, not that she had to. But since the clues had started pointing to her shop, a certain guilt washed over her, despite the fact Donnelly had told her twice now that he knew she was innocent.

"I found the body."

"You found the body." His voice was flat, incredulous.

She nodded.

"And you took pictures, why?"

Good question. She'd been asking herself that since the first one. "I know. It was dumb. Curiosity got the better of me. I took a couple and then asked myself why? I started to delete them and ended up with what you just saw. I was going to delete them when I got home, but never got around to it."

"Is that what has you stressed out?"

Sassy chuffed lightly and told Liam everything. Well, not everything. She left out the part about Donnelly's comment about the handcuffs and the other personal things. She focused on what was really bothering her—one of the clues leading back to her salon and the fact that one of her customers could be a murderer. She hated looking at everyone with suspicion.

When she was done, Liam sat in silence for a long while, his gaze out to sea. She was sure he wished right at this moment that he was out on his boat and a long way from here. From this.

When he turned his gaze back to her, he asked, "What can I do to help?"

She released a long breath, not realizing she'd been holding it. "I don't know if there's anything you can do, but I appreciate the offer." She flicked her gaze toward the cottage. "And for the respite."

He put an arm around her and pulled her into his side. "You know you're welcome any time." A moment later, he pulled away and took her phone from her hand. He switched it on and hit the gallery icon to bring up the crime scene photos. He scanned through them again, paying close attention to the man's face. "I might know him."

Sassy heart jolted erratically. "What?"

"Maybe. It's really hard to tell. I don't see him very often, and I've never seen him dead before . . . the coloring here makes him look . . ."

"Dead?" she finished.

"I was going to say unnatural, but yeah, dead works."

"Who do you think he is?"

"Gustav Kozlow."

Chapter Nine

"If he's the man I'm thinking of, everyone just calls him Gus. He's a Polish blow-in. He worked on boats at home but came to Ireland at the tail end of the recession and picked up jobs here and there until he signed on with the Osprey about six months ago. They went out to sea nearly a week ago with a full crew." He gazed back at the photo of the dead man's face. "Maybe this isn't Gus. I don't know."

"Can we contact the boat? See if this Gus is part of the crew?" The boats had radios, and these days, even mobile phones got signals out at sea. "If he's on the boat, we'll know this isn't Gus. If he's not on the boat, then Detective Donnelly will have a possible identity."

Liam nodded. "Let's pack up. I've got the skipper's number at home. I'll give him a ring."

Back at the cottage, Liam clicked the disconnect on his phone. "He's not picking up. It's keeps diverting to voicemail."

"Can we radio the boat? Maybe he doesn't have his phone on him, or it's too noisy to hear it ring."

Liam nodded. "Sure. Let me fire up the radio."

A few minutes later, Liam had only been able to reach one boat, the Caspian, and they hadn't seen the Osprey, nor could they hail her. Sassy again suspected they just didn't hear the phone or radio calls. But the Caspian's skipper put the word out he was trying to reach the Osprey's skipper as soon as possible. He'd cast a net out to all the nearby boats and hope one of them caught something.

"That's all we can do, Sass. Until we hear from the Osprey,

we can just assume Gus is on board." Liam went into the kitchen and filled the kettle. "Coffee?"

She nodded and watched him pull out grounds and the coffee press. She sat at the tiny kitchen table and wrung her hands together.

"I feel kind of helpless. I hate just waiting."

He leaned back against the counter and folded his arms in front of him. "I know, but let's give it a little time. See if the Caspian can hail the Osprey, or find someone who can. If not, I'll give the Coast Guard a ring and see if they can help. They have longer range radios."

She sat upright in her chair. "Why can't we contact them now?"

"The Coast Guard is for emergencies. Technically, this isn't an emergency. Either Gus is on the boat, or he's dead. Neither of which constitute an emergency."

He was right. She sat back, defeat washing through her.

The kettle clicked off, and her brother prepared their coffee before bringing the mugs to the table. He sat across from her after setting milk and sugar between them.

An hour later and both the radio and Liam's mobile remained silent. Sassy leapt from her chair to pace the tiny kitchen. The waiting was killing her.

"Would it make you feel better to ring the detective with Gus' name? Maybe he'll have better luck than us." Liam's voice remained calm. His suggestion was both a good one and one that made her nervous. Until now, Donnelly had come to her. She'd never rung him.

"Yeah, I could do that," she said, hesitating.

"You sound unsure."

"I'm fine. You're right. If I ring him with Gus' name and the other information, he can do his detective thing. Maybe he'll have better luck with the Coast Guard, if nothing else." She had her phone on her, but Donnelly's card was in her purse. "Be right back."

Sassy closed the guestroom door. If she was going to ring

Donnelly, she didn't want to be any more nervous than she already was. She didn't need Liam hovering over her. With shaking fingers, she opened the phone app and tapped on Donnelly's number. He answered after two rings.

"Miss O'Brien." She heard unmistakable pleasure in his voice. "This is a surprise."

"For me too."

"I hope a pleasurable surprise."

"You'll have to be the judge of that. How did you know it was me?"

"I saved your contact info into my phone, so your name came up."

"What did you do that for? Because this is an ongoing investigation and you need to reach me or something?" Her questions were really just a way of stalling. She hated that the murder was the reason she was contacting Donnelly. Not that she was looking for reasons.

She didn't miss his hesitation. "Sure, let's go with that for now."

Sassy laughed lightly. He was so cheeky. It helped lighten her mood a little.

"So, to what do I owe the pleasure of your call?"

Thinking about other reasons she'd rather ring him under, she said, "I think I might have some information for you on the victim."

Donnelly was quiet for a moment. "Tell me about this information. What can you possibly have that we don't?"

"The man's identity." She blurted it out before she could think of a tactful way of telling him.

"Really." He sounded like he didn't believe her. "I'm all ears."

She relayed what she and Liam had talked about. "We thought you might have some pull with the Coast Guard."

He remained silent for a long moment before asking, "Who's 'we'?"

His question caught her off guard. She was prepared for

questions about Gus, not asking who 'we' was. She chuckled lightly. "I just gave you the victim's possible identity and you're only worried who I'm with? Are you jealous?"

"For now, let's call it curious."

She heard lightness in his voice. He had an easy way about him that calmed her. She was grateful. She needed calm right now. But that didn't stop her from baiting him.

"I'm staying with a man in Clogherhead for a couple days."

"Hmm . . . maybe I should be jealous."

"Maybe you should."

"I'll have to meet this man. See for myself if jealousy is warranted."

"Maybe you will."

Donnelly laughed. "How does your man know the victim might be this Gus?"

"He's a boatman and knows just about everyone at Port Oriel."

"I mean, how is he matching Gus' face with the victim?"

Before thinking, she said, "I showed him a picture."

Silence fell between them so heavily she thought she heard it hit the floor.

When Donnelly spoke again, his words came out with deliberation. She was sure he enunciated each word carefully so there was no mistaking what he wanted to know.

"And where did you get photos of the victim?"

"I . . . umm . . . you see . . ." She'd really put her foot in it this time. Taking a deep breath, she said, "I took them while waiting for you to finish your donuts." There was a long pause on the other end of the line. "Curiosity got the better of me, and you seemed to be taking an inordinate amount of time."

"Are you saying you got bored and filled your time by trampling the crime scene?"

"Ohmygod, no! I was very careful, I swear." Oh, God, he was going to arrest her when she got home. She just knew it. "I wasn't bored. Just . . ."

"Just what?" he asked.

"Curious?" The word confess slammed around inside her skull. *Just tell him why you did it.* "I—I love crime drama."

She thought she heard a snicker from his end of the phone. "I know. We talked about it. You like *Bones* and *Criminal Minds.*"

"And *Castle.* I really love *Castle.* I've watched these shows for years. Anyone who loves crime drama can't help wondering what it would be like to be involved in an investigation. I can pick out the bad guy almost as soon as the show starts."

"That could just be poor script writing," he offered.

"Maybe so, but it doesn't mean I'm not curious. While I was waiting at the scene, I kept thinking *What would Beckett do?* It's not every day you find a dead body, so I—"

"Took a few photos of the crime scene."

What could she say? He had her dead to rights.

"One of them was of the victim's face which you showed to your man and now he might recognize him as . . ." He paused briefly. "Gustav Kozlow. Do I have that right?"

She nodded vigorously, even though he couldn't see her. "Yes."

"Okay. I'll make a call to the Coast Guard and see if we can reach the *Osprey.* I'll need to meet with you as soon as possible to get copies of those photos, unless you can email them to me from where you are." He paused. "I'd hate to interrupt time with *your man.*"

Sassy didn't detect any humor in his voice then. Was he really jealous? She should tell him Liam is her brother, but where was the fun in that?

"I appreciate that. Text me your email address and I'll send the photos over right away," she promised.

"Hold on."

She heard some movement on Donnelly's end of the connection and a moment later, her phone signaled that she had a waiting text.

"You should have it now."

"Let me check."

She minimized the phone screen and brought up her texts. Yep, there it was. She filed the email address in her contacts, adding his phone number at the same time, brought up her email program, attached the photos, and hit send.

"Okay, they're on their way. May be a minute or two before they come through. There are about twenty or so."

"You must have been really curious, then?" A moment later he asked, "So . . . having a nice time in Clogherhead?"

"Yes, I love it up here. It's such a small village, it makes Bettystown look like a metropolis."

"I bet."

"Listen, I don't know why I care, but are you angry I didn't tell you about the photos? I was going to delete them when I got home that day but never got around to it." She did know why she cared what he thought but she wasn't going to tell him. He was already full of himself.

"I don't know if I'm angry or not. Surprised, yes. Absolutely. You've struck me as a woman who wants nothing to do with this. Yet, you took some twenty photos of the crime scene. Maybe you're just too curious for your own good and need some monitoring. I should have a talk with your man about that," he suggested.

Sassy laughed outright. "Doubt that will help. He's never been able to tame me."

She left that statement hanging as she disconnected the call.

Chapter Ten

Sassy had no choice but to let her phone divert to voice mail. Her rubber-glove clad hands were soaked in hair dye, her customer's treatment only half done. She couldn't stop now or the woman's color would be ruined. Donnelly would have to wait.

Again she let the phone divert when it rang a second time.

When the phone rang a third time, her customer laughed. "Someone must really need you, Sassy."

She brushed dye onto the next bit of hair to even out the woman's naturally graying hair. "He'll have to wait, Mrs. Murphy. I'll not have your color uneven."

"He?" The woman's interest piqued.

Mrs. Kelly spun in the chair beside Mrs. Murphy and said, "You never told us you were seeing anyone."

A plastic-wrapped head peaked from around the mirror on the opposite work station. "Sassy's dating? Good for you, girl." This came from Widow Doyle.

Sassy chuffed lightly. Why was her love life so interesting to everyone around her?

Just then, Mrs. Ellison stepped through the door and their gazes met. Sassy didn't realize she had an appointment, but was thankful she moved to the waiting area without comment.

"I'm not dating him or anyone. He's just a friend." Sassy refocused her gaze on Mrs. Murphy's hair, hoping the ladies would let the subject drop. Mary's snicker from beside her forced a warning glare at her friend to keep quiet. Mary settled Mrs. Kelly back in her seat to continue with her cut. But that didn't stop the ladies chatter.

Fortunately, Widow Doyle sat back in her chair too, but it didn't stop her from pressing the subject. "Just a friend, eh? I don't believe it. I heard about a young man coming into the salon last week. I'll bet that's him."

Sassy thought she heard a hint of satisfaction from the woman.

"I heard about that too, Agnes," said Mrs. Kelly. "I even heard they were seen together at Chutney."

Great. I'm a topic of village gossip.

Keeping her nose down and her gaze on Mrs. Murphy's hair, she reminded them, "Just friends, ladies."

Was Donnelly a friend? Probably not, technically speaking, but it should have been a reasonable answer to get these ladies to change the subject.

The ladies laughed.

"Fiona said you two were sitting very close for a long time over at the café last week. She said it looked very intimate." Mrs. Murphy added, elongating the word intimate as if it was a bad thing.

"Fiona is a worse gossip than the lot of you put together," Sassy said, trying to control the irritation in her voice.

Widow Doyle peaked around the mirror again and said, "I hear he's an investigator working on that murder."

Sassy's breath caught, forcing a choke out of her. She kept her hands moving and tried not reacting. She did pay close attention, though, to where the conversation was going.

Mrs. Murphy gasped. "Oh, that was dreadful. The poor man. Have they identified him yet?"

"No, I don't think so," said Mrs. Kelly.

Mrs. Murphy added, "Well, if that young man is a detective, I'm sure he'll be the one to solve it. He seems very diligent."

"I heard they set up a special incident room in Laytown just for this case. He drives in every day from Ashbourne," Mrs. Kelly said.

Mrs. Murphy caught Sassy's gaze in the mirror in front of them and said, "I'm surprised you haven't let him stay in your guestroom, Sassy. If you really are just friends." To her horror, the woman winked at her.

That's it! Sassy stripped off her gloves, now finished with the dye, and tossed them on her work trolley. Trying to keep the annoyance out of her voice, she said, "Let this set for a minute, Mrs. Murphy, and then we'll finish up." With that, she spun on her heals and headed for the door to her flat upstairs.

As she stomped away, she caught Mrs. Ellison's gaze but didn't stop to chat with her. She needed a moment to herself. But when she heard Mrs. Murphy say, "I bet she's going to ring him now," Sassy decided to take as long as she needed.

Mary stopped her at the door. "Sassy. Maybe you should tell them," she whispered.

She cast a glare across the room then back to Mary. "I'm already village gossip. Can you imagine what would happen if they knew?"

"I know, but at least you wouldn't be forced to defend yourself. Who knows, maybe these women know something your detective hasn't discovered yet. You know how busybodies are."

Sassy looked over the ladies again and shook her head. She gazed into Mary's eyes. "I think the man has already been identified. That's probably why Donnelly was trying to reach me. I need to go up and ring him." Then added, "Where it's quiet."

Mary's features changed to understanding and patted her arm. "No worries. I'll see what Mrs. Ellison wants. And if you're not back in half an hour, I'll finish Mrs. Murphy for you. Her dye will have set by then."

Sassy laughed. "And if I don't return, I'm sure Mrs. Murphy will be well-vindicated in her assumption that there's more to my relationship with Donnelly than just being friends." She closed the door behind her and took the stairs by twos.

Before ringing Donnelly, she looked at the time and decided she had a moment to take Bracken for a quick stroll. They both needed the fresh air.

On her return, she met the detective in her kitchen. Bracken growled and held her stance just inside the door when she saw him. Sassy's heart leapt into her throat at the fright.

"How did you get up here?" she gasped. "Whisht," she said to the dog and moved through the kitchen to put her in her bed in the sitting room. Donnelly followed her.

"Mary let me in. When I couldn't get you on the phone, I came over. We need to talk."

Great, now he knew where she lived. Not that it was a secret, but it was supposed to be her sanctuary.

She took him back into the kitchen. The sitting room was too casual. She wasn't ready to be casual with Donnelly. She flipped on the kettle and set two cups on the table for coffee.

"Sit," she ordered. She was oddly pleased that he obeyed.

By the time she was finished taking out the items she needed—coffee press, grounds, milk, sugar, spoons, biscuits—the kettle clicked off. She filled the press with water and watched it turn black before setting it on the table.

She sat across from Donnelly, but still refused to look at him as she prepared the coffee—plunging the press then filling their cups.

She finally gazed up and saw he was intently watching her. "What?"

"You do the silent treatment very well," he noted.

"What do you expect? I come into my home and see you standing here. You scared the crap out of me, for starters. And secondly, you weren't invited up here."

"Mary showed me up."

"It's not Mary's place now, is it?"

Donnelly chuckled. "No, I guess not. But how did I know you live here and it's not just part of your shop?"

After a moment's realization, she chuckled. "Some detective."

Donnelly poured a drop of milk into his cup before tasting it. "Funny you should say that."

"Why's that?" After stirring her lashing of milk and sugar, she reached for a biscuit.

Donnelly shifted in his chair. He seemed agitated about something, but she remained silent until he was ready to tell her. Had they reached the Coast Guard? Was the victim really Gus Kozlow? She started shaking a little.

Finally, he said, "Turns out you just may be a better investigator than all of us combined."

That was not what she expected to hear. Surely, he was teasing. "Maybe we should switch jobs, then."

He grunted. "By the looks of things, you can hold down both jobs."

He was all business today, so she waited until he was ready to talk to her.

"We rang the Coast Guard, but they couldn't get through to the Osprey. They think the boat may have gone into the North Atlantic somewhere, so they're sending helicopters out to find the boat. Meanwhile, Coast Guards from Scotland and Iceland are also trying to radio them."

"Seems to me it shouldn't be this difficult reaching a fishing boat in this day and age," she remarked.

"Normally, it isn't."

"Okay, then, why are you here? You could have texted me."

It was then she saw a folder on the table. He must have set it there when he came in, and in all the excitement of finding him in her home, she hadn't seen it until now.

He pulled out some photo printouts she recognized from those she'd taken. He pointed to the one she'd taken of the victim's collar. "Did you see this when you took this photo?" She nodded when he pointed to the piece of plastic drying into the blood.

He chuckled lightly but she didn't hear any humor in it. "Well, turns out that our crack forensics team missed it. We don't have a single photo of this item. And it was missed again when he was stripped for autopsy."

Sassy sat back in her chair and folded her arms in front of her, taking in this bit of information. "Huh," was all she could say.

"This piece of evidence was recovered from the victim's clothes over the weekend and sent for analysis." She watched him pull out a printout that looked a lot like the one he'd shown her last week with results about the hair dye. He slid it in front of her.

She looked up at him. "What was it?"

"Turns out, it's a long piece of acrylic—a fake fingernail—that broke off during what we're now thinking was a struggle."

She pushed the paper away from her and sat back. "And you're here to tell me this is another piece of evidence that points to me? Really, Detective, you're starting to give me a complex."

He chuffed. "Fortunately for you, the results came back that it's generic acrylic used in the mass production of false nails. Even the color on the nail is from a common brand called Oh, My!." He looked at a second set of test results. "The color was Oh, My! Vixen Red. This brand and the color are widely available."

"We also use it in our salon." Even though the polish was considered generic or popular, it was still another piece of evidence pointing in her direction, and she told him so.

"While this is true, there's one thing that doesn't point in your direction."

"What's that?"

"DNA from a second person."

Well, that was an unexpected revelation. "Are you sure it wasn't mine? I walked all around the body . . . when I first arrived to see if he was alive and then to take some pictures."

Donnelly held out his hands in her direction. "Give me your hands."

She hesitated, then reached out to him. His warm palms

gently pulled her toward him. She gazed into his eyes and wondered what he was up to.

"Look." He indicated for her to look at their hands joined. She felt her cheeks warm at his continued touch. "Your nails are short. My guess is so you can cut hair more easily. The nail we found was acrylic, broken where the rough end was ripped from the woman's finger. That's where we found the DNA."

Sassy cringed and gazed up again. "Ripped from her finger? Sounds painful. Are you sure it's a woman?"

"We're assuming this is a female. Unless you can give me evidence that men also wear fake nails."

She had to think. While she didn't have any male clients, she didn't think any of her girls had any either. She couldn't remember the last time she'd seen a man wear acrylics . . . unless they were press-ons for drag performances like those she'd seen in the city.

She shook her head. "None in my salon."

Donnelly nodded curtly. "We're still waiting for the DNA results to come back, but we're going with a theory now. A man and woman met on the beach, there was a struggle, and she killed him before fleeing the scene."

She shivered. "Do you think he was trying to rape her?"

"Unlikely, since it was out in the open where anyone could see them. We don't know the circumstances, but until we can reach the Osprey to confirm if the victim is who you think he may be, and until we get the DNA results back, it's all just conjecture."

"Thanks for sharing this with me. I know you didn't have to."

"Well . . ."

Uh-oh. "Well, what?"

"Have you or one of your employees repaired any nails in the last week? Or has anyone been in with a finger injury? This wouldn't have bled a lot, but would be quite painful. Even still, her ego might have still wanted the nail repaired," he suggested.

Shaking her head, "No, not that I know of. I don't do nails myself, but I'll ask our nail artist, Finola."

"I appreciate that."

"I'm curious, why do you think this woman has an ego?"

"Just guessing. That hair dye doesn't come cheap, and she wears well-manicured nails. Just two clues to a woman who's well turned out. Egos come with being posh . . . or putting on airs."

Sassy laughed. "All right, I'll keep my eyes open for an airy woman with a broken fingernail."

Donnelly's smile reached his eyes. "Thanks, and I'll let you know if we hear back from the Coast Guard. Meanwhile, maybe your man will let us know if the Osprey makes it back to port before we can reach them by radio or chopper."

"Will do."

They sat together for a long moment gazing at each other. Was he waiting for her to say something, or was he building up to another revelation? Oddly, she didn't feel uncomfortable sitting like this with him.

Donnelly still held her hands in his. There was gentleness in his gaze. His thumb rubbed the back of her hand. It sent a shiver rushing through her, and her heart beat a little quicker. She really should tell him Liam was her brother.

As she opened her mouth to speak, there was a knock on the interior door to her flat. Sassy jerked back, her hands falling away from Donnelly's. "Sorry." She stood up and went to find Mary at the door.

A moment later, she was back in the kitchen. "I'm sorry. I need to get back into the salon. Thanks again for sharing your evidence with me. I know you don't have to, but I appreciate it."

He collected his folder and papers off the table and stood gazing at her for another long moment without speaking. Then with a nod, he showed himself out the backdoor.

As soon as the door closed behind him, she released a long, deep breath. What was that man doing to her insides?

Chapter Eleven

"What the hell is wrong with people," Sassy asked Mary as they walked across the road to SuperSaver. They needed a few items for the salon kitchen for the other girls' breaks, and Mary accompanied her, as she needed to post a letter in the small post office in the back of the little supermarket.

"What do you mean?" Mary looked around them, but didn't seem to find anything out of the ordinary.

"Look, there's another one." She smiled and dipped her head to acknowledge obvious gawkers. "Everyone is staring at me."

Mary laughed. "I'm sure you're just imagining it."

"I'm telling you, they're staring. Watch as we walk."

Her friend casually looked around while they walked. "Wow. You're right. I wonder what that's all about?"

"I don't know, but it's making me nervous. You didn't tell anyone I found that damn body, did you?" She couldn't keep the irritation from her voice.

Mary stopped her at the entrance into the supermarket. "I promised I wouldn't. You know me better than that."

Feeling deflated, Sassy said, "You're right. I'm sorry. I just hate this. I wish the investigation would wrap up sooner rather than later so my life can get back to normal."

A few minutes later, they met Fiona at the checkout. "Hi, Mary. Sassy," she coolly greeted them.

Sassy had never liked Fiona. Not even when she had been dating her brother. When she had called it off with Seamus six months ago, she felt doubly relieved to be rid of him, and Fiona. While the woman had never done anything outright to her, Fiona was smug and interfering, more so than any typical busybody.

Her memory rocketed back to the discussion in her salon a few days ago, when Mrs. Murphy said Fiona had been talking about Sassy and the man in the café. A rock settled in the pit of her stomach.

"Fiona," she greeted with snipped courtesy and turned to wait for her turn the queue.

"I hear that detective was back in your place again on Monday."

Sassy ignored the accusatory sounding statement.

"Rumor has it you're sleeping with him." Fiona's words and aggressive tone forced Sassy to turn around again.

Heads turned in their direction, or at the very least, cocked to the side so eavesdroppers could hear better.

She chose her words carefully. "And how is what I do any of your business?" Her gaze bore into the woman, challenging her to continue in front of witnesses. Sassy folded her arms in front of her to help prevent her from punching Fiona in the face, not that she was a violent woman.

Fiona paid no attention to the gathering looks. "Seamus might have something to say about it."

"Really? We broke up over six months ago. He has no say over my life. Neither do you, so I would appreciate if you would butt out. And stop spreading rumors around the village. It makes you look shallow." Sassy moved to turn away from Fiona, but the woman's hand was on her arm, keeping her in place. Using great restraint and careful word choices, she slowly moved her gaze from the offending hand up Fiona's arm to her face. She enunciated each word slowly. "Don't you dare touch me."

Fiona released her arm, but didn't back down.

"Seamus said you were a slut."

Sassy refused to be baited so kept quiet, but her gaze

remained firmly on Fiona. She wouldn't back down either. She had no reason to defend herself. She'd done nothing wrong. Other than agreeing to date Seamus in the first place. She had known he was from a rough family, but he'd been charming and fun. He was all laughs . . . until she disagreed with him or he thought she was flirting with other men.

She shivered inside remembering the first time he'd hit her. It had also been the last.

"Maybe you were the one who killed that man up in Mornington. I heard that too, and that's why the detective keeps going in to see you."

Sassy felt her brows draw together but still didn't say anything.

"Maybe you're sleeping with that detective, hoping he won't arrest you. Seamus said that would be just like you."

Why was Fiona behaving this way? She was normally just a busybody in the worse sense of the word—someone who enjoyed stirring the proverbial pot just to create some excitement around her. But this was going too far.

Sassy turned to the checkout clerk. "I'm sorry. I'll be back later for these." With her head held high and her shoulders back, she walked through the small throng of onlookers and out the door.

"Mrs. Ellison." Sassy acknowledged the startled woman at the doors. She wanted to run back to her shop, but kept as steady a pace as possible, hoping to prove to . . . who, the villagers? . . . that she was unruffled by the encounter. Really, she didn't care what they thought, but her forced restraint had to quell some of the rumors Fiona was starting or had been throwing around.

Taking the back stairs by twos, she slammed the door behind her and rushed into her bedroom where she flung herself on the bed and cried. Bracken inched her lumbering frame onto the bed and laid beside her, her snout pushing between Sassy's elbows so she could lick her mistress' chin. Sassy wrapped her arms around the dog and sobbed into her furry neck.

She wasn't crying because of Fiona.

She wasn't crying because of Seamus and what he'd done to her.

She wasn't even crying because, for a while, she'd been a suspect in a murder.

It was a combination of everything. She didn't like drama, or complications, or anything stressful. That's what she loved about living in a small village . . . the peace. Even if everyone seemed to know everyone else's business, it was at least peaceful.

But this last week had been the kind of stress no one should have to face. And Fiona's unprovoked attack made it all boil over. Like a kettle letting off steam, she let herself cry rather than risking a criminal record for putting her fist through the woman's teeth. No matter how satisfying she thought it might feel.

A knock on the interior door forced her off the bed. It would be Mary checking up on her. That's the kind of friend Mary was.

"You okay, sweetie?" she asked, her friend rubbing her upper arm.

She nodded. "Yes, thanks, Mary." She walked into the sitting room, Mary following her. Sassy paced, her arms crossed in front of her, trying to figure out what had gotten into Fiona. "What was that woman thinking? All this time and she chooses now to have a go off me. Why? To what end?"

"Her whole family is trouble. I'm glad you got out when you did. What Seamus did to you was unforgiveable, and Fiona had no cause to attack you the way she did."

Sassy couldn't add anything to Mary's statement. Seamus had been a bastard, and she was lucky she was a smart enough woman to leave at the first hint of trouble. She knew some women stuck around hoping to change their man. But men didn't change. Especially men like Seamus.

"Hey, I bought those things you left on the conveyor. No

need to go back. At least not today."

She looked up at her friend and smiled weakly. "Thanks. Just take the money from petty cash to reimburse yourself."

"Already sorted. Is there anything I can do for you? I looked at your schedule. I can take on a couple of your clients, and I can call in another girl to cover the rest."

Confusion spun through her. She could do with being away from gossips for the rest of the day, but on the other hand, the work was a great distraction.

"Thanks, I'll be fine. I can't hide up here forever. Besides, if I don't come down now, Fiona will have won. And customers will start talking . . . more than they already are. I don't need the added hassle."

Mary rubbed her arm again. A minor comfort, but an appreciated one. "Are you sure?" she asked.

Sassy nodded.

"All right, then. I'll see you down there soon. No rush."

"Thanks, Mary. I appreciate it."

She closed the door behind her friend then leaned back on it, sighing.

Sassy had been asking herself Why me? a lot lately. A little voice in the back of her mind said, Why not you? It has to be someone.

"Great. Just great."

Chapter Twelve

As the weekend approached, the villagers paid less attention to her on the street, which she appreciated. What struck her oddly was the number of salon bookings. The sudden increased clients meant she had started working her staff full time, rather than alternating part-time hours between them.

Sassy laughed at the irony. She was sure Fiona was hoping to destroy Sassy's credibility, but instead had boosted her business. *Thanks, Fiona!*

Sassy now waited for a new customer to come in for her appointment when her phone rang. Donnelly. She considered letting it divert to voicemail, but knowing him, he'd just show up again if he couldn't reach her.

"Good afternoon, Detective." Sassy moved into the narrow hall leading toward the kitchen for some privacy.

"Good afternoon, Miss O'Brien." Sassy heard the levity in his voice. "I hear there was some excitement around yours this week."

"News travels quickly, doesn't it?"

"Yes, especially when a retired inspector's wife was in the supermarket at the time."

Sassy laughed. "Gotta love a small village. So, to what do I owe the honor of this call? Please tell me your case is wrapped up now, and I can go back to my lonely, boring life."

"No such luck. But I did want to ask if you're free to meet up. There is news on the case I wanted to share with you," he said.

She felt her brows draw together with curiosity. "Can't you just tell me on the phone?"

"I could, but I enjoy your company."

"And it doesn't appear to bother you about my man?" She liked teasing him.

"I'd say if things became awkward between us, you can well handle yourself. If nothing else, I am a gentleman and respect your relationship," he said, unconvincingly. "Besides, there's nothing wrong with friends having a coffee together, is there?"

"You think we're friends?"

"Isn't that's what you told the ladies in your salon?"

Wait a minute. He wasn't in her salon during that conversation. How did he know? Was Mary feeding him information? Confused, she just said, "I guess it's true then. You know how gossip has its roots in truth."

"Funny. Will you meet me?"

Sassy thought for a moment. What harm would it be?

"Sure, but I can't leave now. After Fiona's outburst in the supermarket the other day, we've suddenly become very busy. I don't know if the new customers are just curious for more gossip, but it's a great opportunity to build our clientele," she told him.

"Congratulations on the new business."

"Thanks. My last customer is at six o'clock. I can meet you after. Say . . . around seven o'clock?"

Donnelly didn't hesitate. "Sure, that's grand. See you then."

As agreed, Donnelly was on her doorstep precisely at seven o'clock. Her last customer was a quick trim, so Sassy spent the last half hour cleaning the salon. The detective had arrived a bit early, but rather than come in, he waited outside until their agreed time. He leaned against the short wall around the front of her place, his back to her, watching things going on around him in the village. Always vigilant, she suspected.

When she was ready, she leaned out the door. "Detective." Donnelly spun around and smiled, rising to move toward her. "I need to take Bracken out for a walk. Come with us?"

"Sure."

She showed him up to her flat through the interior entrance. Bracken growled under her breath at the sight of a stranger in her home, but Sassy quickly quieted the dog. "Here," she said, handing Donnelly a couple dog biscuits. "She'll be your friend forever if you give her these." Turning to the dog she said, "Bracken, sit."

Donnelly laughed behind her. "How can you keep a pony in such a small space?"

Sassy looked around. "It's not that small. I've two bedrooms, the loo, a sizable kitchen, and sitting room, plus a small pantry. It's just the two of us so there's plenty of room. It helps we live beside the sea. I enjoy running, and so does she. Don't let her size fool you. Just because she's one of the tallest dogs in the world, wolfhounds are also notoriously just as happy to lounge by the fire."

Donnelly chuckled. "I'll take your word for it. So, how do I give these to her without her taking off my hand?"

"Here, do it this way." She put a biscuit on her open left palm and let Bracken see it. "Bracken, shake." The dog lifted her paw and Sassy gave it a little shake. "Good girl." The dog lapped up the biscuit, sweeping her tail across the hardwood floor. "Now you do it."

He did as she had, putting the biscuit on the palm of his left hand and showed it to the dog. At Sassy's quick nod, the detective said, "Bracken, shake" and held out his free hand. The dog remained still. "Bracken, shake." Still, the dog remained in place.

"Bracken, okay," said Sassy, giving the dog permission.

The dog lifted her paw and waited for Donnelly to take it. Laughing, he shook the dog's paw and offered the biscuit, which was lapped up quickly. "She didn't even chew it." He took the second biscuit and shook Bracken's paw again. The dog allowed him to scratch her head before she scampered off, returning a moment later with her lead.

Sassy grabbed the lead. "Good girl." She snapped it onto the dog's collar. Turning to Donnelly. "You don't mind talking while we walk. She's been cooped up most of the day."

"Sure. Lead the way."

As soon as they were on the beach, Sassy let Bracken off the lead and tossed the ball she'd pocketed on the way out the door. The dog chased it across the sand and brought it back as they walked.

She gave the ball to Donnelly. "The best way to make friends with her . . . second to biscuits."

Sassy enjoyed the comfortable companionship with Donnelly. Watching him play with Bracken seemed natural. The dog didn't easily accept new people into her life, especially men, but she really seemed to like the detective.

Sassy thought she really liked the detective too.

Her belly fluttered, remembering his touch on her cheek and how it seemed so natural when he held her hands in his. He calmed her—warmed her from the inside. She felt the urge to hold his hand now as they strolled along the sandy strand, but stuffed her hands into her coat pockets instead. He was only here investigating a murder. Sure, they got on well and he was fun to tease, but once the case was closed, he'd be gone. No sense getting too close.

"So, what was this information you wanted to share with me?" she asked, pulling her thoughts away from something that would never happen. If anything could happen. She was still gun shy from what Seamus had done.

Keeping his focus on the dog and throwing the ball for her, he said, "The Coast Guard finally got in touch with the Osprey."

Sassy halted and stared up at Donnelly, her heart suddenly pounding. "You couldn't tell me on the phone? I could have at least sat down for this."

He took her elbow, guided her up the beach to dry sand,

and pulled her down to sit beside him.

"Tell me," she finally said. She couldn't be any readier for what he was about to tell her.

She gazed up at him. He looked at her, but didn't say anything. She enjoyed looking at him, and by his gentle expression, he must like looking at her too. He did it enough. *What's he thinking?* The answer that came to her was a familiar one . . . tell him Liam is your brother. She would, but this wasn't the time.

He inhaled deeply. "The Osprey had been far out in the North Sea since just before you found the body. The skipper said Gustav Kozlow never made it on board."

Chapter Thirteen

"Ohmygod," was all she could say.

She wasn't surprised. Not really. Liam had a great memory, so if he thought the man in her pictures was Gus, she immediately accepted he was. Donnelly's confirmation that Gus wasn't on the Osprey meant the victim had to be the missing fisherman.

"What now? Have you formally identified the victim then?"

"The Osprey's skipper gave us the address he had on file for Gus and we carried out a search yesterday afternoon," he said.

"Tell me you found something to help find his killer." She started shaking. Was it the chilly evening breeze, or was she just anxious about the situation? She wanted Donnelly to tell her the man had been identified and clues now led to the capture of his killer.

To be honest, it scared her that such a violent person was out there and living in the community.

She shivered again, her thoughts flashing back to Seamus. She prayed he wasn't involved. His violence was the reason she'd left him, but was he a killer? God, she hoped not.

What about the fake nail and the hair? It didn't make sense if Seamus was involved. But what about Fiona?

"He's been living under the radar in a small caravan up near Clogherhead. He only uses the place when the Osprey is docked at Port Oriel between trips. He pays rent by the month in cash because he spends most of the season out at sea. He can easily come and go that way. When he didn't show up by the time the boat was ready to cast off the lines, the skipper assumed Gus was staying behind to spend time with his girlfriend. Apparently, the previous trip had lasted longer than expected and Gus was anxious to stay behind this trip to spend time with the woman. There's no lack of boat hands waiting for work, so Gus was easily replaced and the Osprey was free to leave on time with a full crew."

"Didn't any of his neighbors miss seeing him?"

"Apparently not. When he hadn't been seen at the caravan, they assumed he was at sea."

As Donnelly talked, it didn't skip Sassy's notice how he had scooted closer to her. His nearness comforted her, as did his body heat.

"We weren't surprised by how sparse the caravan was, especially considering the little time he spent there. We didn't find his passport or much in the way of personal belongings, other than a few clothes, but we did find an address in Poland which the team is chasing up for next of kin. The only photo we found was of a man and woman together at the circus, which we assume was the one that came through Bettystown a few months ago."

She was instantly cold when he leaned away from her to pull out a photo from his jacket's inner pocket to show her. She took it and scanned the image for details. Yes, the man looked like the victim—the same big man with dark, shaggy hair and round face. The couple held each other closely, side-by-side, as if they had been stopped while walking to have the photo taken, something common at the larger carnivals. They were both smiling with the carnival lights behind them, bright against a fading sky. They looked . . . happy. What had gone wrong?

Sassy gazed at the woman—dark, shoulder-length wavy hair, short in stature against Gus' taller frame but she had a full figure. Being a member of a small community, everyone knew each other, even if just by sight. Sassy should have known her.

"This woman looks familiar, but I can't place her. Something around the eyes, but . . . I don't know. He definitely looks like the victim though."

Donnelly put the photo back in his pocket. "We think so too, but we're waiting for the fingerprints to come back to make an official identification. Meanwhile, we're looking into known associates . . . anyone who might have had a grudge."

"What about the woman? Are you searching for her too?" she asked.

Donnelly nodded. "Of course. There were a few sets of prints in the caravan; forensics are trying to match them now. We're sure one of them belongs to Gus, and we're hoping the others lead us to the woman in the photo."

"Did the Osprey skipper know who Gus was seeing?"

He shook his head. "No. Just that she wasn't from Clogherhead. Gus didn't have a car so he used the bus or walked when he couldn't get a lift. The skipper said he thought Gus always travelled south, which makes sense since he was found in Mornington."

"I'm sorry."

Donnelly leaned away and looked down at her. "For what? You have nothing to be sorry for."

"I should recognize the woman. She has lovely hair, and there aren't many salons in the area. It's one of three between Bettystown and Laytown, or she'd go into Drogheda. Even if she didn't come into my salon, I should recognize her. You know how familiar villages can be."

"Don't worry about it. We'll find her, and we'll solve this case. I'd like to say I have a feeling it'll wrap soon, but solving a case can never be predicted. I do think the woman in the photo may be the key though. If she's the girlfriend, hopefully she can shed some light on things we may be missing . . . know someone who wanted Gus dead, or at least badly hurt. She may have witnessed an altercation between Gus and someone else, or even witnessed his murder."

The last hung heavily on the air. Sassy hoped the woman hadn't seen her lover killed before her eyes. The terror she must have felt, if she had. The helplessness at not being able to stop it. She tried suppressing another shiver at the thought. She took comfort in Donnelly's nearness and fought not to sink into him.

They sat quietly together for a long while. Neither seemed in a hurry to move.

Heat rose up between them where their bodies touched. Donnelly's scent filled her senses, pushing away the direction their conversation had gone. He felt so natural against her . . . familiar. As if her body recognized something long lost in him. The heat of him where he touched her felt right. Everything about him screamed YES.

Should she be feeling these things after only knowing him for such a short time?

She was glad things were starting to move forward with the case. In a way, though, she hoped the case was never solved because it would keep Donnelly closer to Bettystown. Closer to her.

But in reality, Gus probably had family back home who would want to know what happened to him. And if he was still with the girl in the picture, surely she'd want to know too. Sassy knew if it was her, she'd want to know.

Life could be so complicated.

Sassy watched Bracken's innocent, carefree play at the water's edge, bouncing back when the water lapped at her feet and then chased it back out to sea with fake ferocious snaps. Sassy wondered what a truly carefree life could be like for herself.

Chapter Fourteen

T*ell him about Liam* repeated through her head.
They couldn't keep doing this. It was unfair to both
of them, especially Donnelly since he didn't know the truth.
Teasing him about her man had been fun for a while, but
she now sensed things straining between them. It wasn't
as if they'd started something, but she felt the stirrings of
attraction, and her intuition told her he felt the same.

But even if this was all there was between her and the
detective, she didn't want him going back to Ashbourne
thinking she was a tease, or that he was putting her on a
knife's edge of making her cheat on a boyfriend who didn't
exist.

"Donnelly," she started after taking a deep breath. "I need
to tell you something."

"What's that?" he asked, unmoving.

"It's . . . it's about the man in Clogherhead."

"You mean Gus?"

She paused a moment. "No. Mine." She felt Donnelly
stiffen beside her, but he still didn't move away from her.

"We're just friends, Miss O'Brien. We're not doing
anything wrong." He looked down at her then, his gaze
penetrating, telling her his words lied to them both.

Reluctantly, she pulled away from him and sat on her
knees, facing at him. The evening chill instantly penetrated
through her now that she wasn't sharing Donnelly's heat.

"I think this is important. You and I need to clear the air
about . . . this." She waved her hands across the space they'd
just shared.

She had his full attention now. His serious gaze replaced
the gentle, comforting one she preferred. "What do you
think this is?" he asked.

"I don't know, but I think you need to know something
about—"

Just then, his mobile phone rang, cutting her off. "Sorry. I have to get this." He didn't move to find privacy for the call, and when she tried moving, he grasped her arm and nodded that it was okay to stay. To give him an illusion of privacy, she turned her gaze toward Bracken who was now loping across the sand with a short piece of driftwood in her grasp.

"Donnelly," she heard him answer. "Uh-huh. Right. Okay." His replies were clipped and more sharply delivered as the call progressed. "Yes. Uh huh . . . Really? All right then. Thanks for the call."

She turned her gaze back to him, ready to continue their conversation. The lie was eating at her more than ever.

Before she could speak again, he said, "That was forensics. Fingerprints from the caravan match our victim. It's official. The victim was Gustav Kozlow."

"Ohdeargod," she gasped. "Okay, I'm not terribly surprised, but thank God he has his identity back." She paused, expecting Donnelly to continue. When he didn't, she asked, "Is there something else?"

He shook his head. "Just trying to piece everything together. We're not getting any hits on the other fingerprints. At least not yet, but since Gus' were the strongest, it made sense to run those first."

"Is there anything I can help with?"

"Do you mind if we head back? I'd like to check my notes. If I have them in front of me, maybe they'll make more sense."

Sassy nodded. "Sure."

She stood up and held out her hand to Donnelly and was surprised he took it as he propelled himself onto his long legs. Smiling, she brushed the sand off her backside and called to Bracken that it was time to go home.

"You've trained her well, Miss O'Brien." He watched Bracken gambol along the strand toward them, the driftwood stick still between her teeth.

"Thanks. She's a fun dog."

Donnelly had parked his car behind the salon rather than leave it on the street on a busy Friday evening. When they arrived, they stopped in the center of the drive with an uncomfortable silence suddenly hanging over them. She still hadn't told him about Liam, but he had new information about the murder he wanted to sift through.

With obvious hesitation in her voice, she asked, "Do you want to bring your paperwork inside? You can look it over while I make us something for dinner."

He thought for a moment. "I better not, but thank you."

"Are you sure? We still need to talk." She had to tell him about Liam before it went any further.

He nodded. "We do, and I'm really sorry for the interruption. And as much as I'd love to stay, I need to get back into the office and go through the new evidence. I'll pop round tomorrow and we can finish talking then. You'll have my undivided attention," he promised.

She crossed her arms in front of her. "All right. Sorry I couldn't be more help about the woman, but if I hear or see anything, I've got you on speed dial."

There was an awkward moment when she thought Donnelly would kiss her goodbye. She wanted him to, but given the misunderstanding about her brother and the new evidence at the office, a simple parting was probably for the best.

"Thanks. Good night." He turned toward his car.

She watched him pull away before taking Bracken upstairs.

Sassy spun a circle in her sitting room.

Her nerves were getting the better of her. She'd tried twice now to tell Donnelly about Liam and both times they'd been interrupted. She was beginning to think the Fates were playing with her.

She glanced at the television but had no desire to watch anything. Not even her beloved Castle.

She wasn't hungry, and even if she was, she had no desire to cook, and the thought of takeaway made her stomach hurt.

She didn't want to read.

She could turn on the radio or put on a CD and brush the evening sand out of Bracken, but when she found the dog, she was completely panned out. Toes twitching, ears cocking, and soft chuffing meant the dog was out for the evening.

Was she bored? No. But this thing between her and Donnelly had her so agitated, she couldn't think of anything else.

Liam abruptly popped into her head, but not because of anything between her and Donnelly.

She should ring her brother and tell him the news. She hoped he was home on a Friday night, or had at least remembered to take his mobile with him.

The phone rang as Sassy fell back onto the sofa. She hadn't bothered turning on the lights, but let the kitchen light filter into the sitting room. She hoped the ambient light relaxed her, because right now, every time she thought about Donnelly, something came alive and poked at her insides.

When her call diverted to voicemail, she pressed redial and waited again. Liam picked up on the third ring.

"Liam! Finally."

"Hey, Sass."

The cacophony of noise on his end of the line was almost deafening. "You'll have to speak up. I can barely hear you."

"Hang on."

She heard him moving around and then it was much quieter, though she heard the music faintly in the background.

"I've gone outside. The Oriel is busy tonight. The Caspian came back to port today with their biggest ever catch. Drinks all 'round on them . . . all night. Gotta get mine in while I can." She heard his laughter on the line. By the sounds of it, he'd already had a couple pints in him. "What's the craic?"

"You probably already know, but the Coast Guard finally made contact with the Osprey."

Liam was quiet for a moment. "No, I didn't know. Was Gus on board?"

"No, Liam. He wasn't." She told him about the search in his caravan, the fingerprint results, and that they'd now positively identified him as the victim. "I thought you'd want to know."

"Yeah, thanks . . . I guess. Now what?" he asked.

"Donnelly has gone back to his office to do his detective thing. They still don't have the killer, but with the positive identification, they have some better leads to chase up."

Then she remembered the photo. "Hey, they found just one photo in Gus' caravan. It was of him and a dark haired woman. Do you remember seeing anyone with him . . . maybe in the Oriel Pub, or even her just hanging around the harbor? She looks familiar, but I can't place her face."

Liam was quiet for a moment. "There have been a couple women, but I don't know if any of them were very serious. He pretty much stuck with other Poles in the area when he was between jobs. I think they went into Drogheda as a group a few times."

"Well, that's something else I can slide Donnelly's way. Anyway, I'm glad that part of the mystery has been solved. It seemed so sad the victim didn't have an identity . . . or at least a known identity. Hopefully, it'll be over soon, and we can all get back to our normal, boring lives in Bettystown."

"Boring? Right." She heard him chuff. "I heard Seamus' sister caused a stir recently."

"Dammit. It's bad enough there are busybodies in the village, but now gossip is village hopping? How did you hear about it?" She didn't bother disguising the irritation in her voice.

"Mary."

Just the one name said it all. "Dammit," she repeated. "Why would she tell you that?"

Liam chuckled. "Well, I'm guessing A, she has a crush on me and just wanted a reason to ring, or B, she knew you wouldn't tell me yourself. My guess is B, though A seems probable too."

"Great."

"Based on your response, you weren't going to say anything."

"It was an isolated incident. I'm a better person than she is, so I walked away. Oddly, her public outburst has nearly doubled my current bookings. Ain't karma great?" She laughed then sucked it up, remembering her hectic schedule tomorrow. No more casual Saturdays for her. As long as there was business, she couldn't afford to take extra time off.

"Well, I'm glad Mary told me. If Seamus rears his ugly head, we'll know where it started this time."

"Here's hoping that was the end of it. I've got enough problems of my own. I don't need her, or him, on top of them. People need to accept and move on."

"I can't fault you there. I better find the Caspian skipper and give him the news. Even though Gus wasn't Irish, he was still one of our own up here. It's likely the skipper will want to be the one to tell everyone himself. Thanks for letting me know."

"No worries. We'll talk soon. Love you."

"Love you too. Give that pony a scratch on the head for me."

Chapter Fifteen

She didn't think she'd ever feel grateful for a Monday coming around.

Saturday had passed quickly with her full schedule. The rapid turnover of customers kept her thoughts about Donnelly not checking in with her out of her mind.

As had happened when the news of a body being found a little over two weeks ago, the village gossip was now about him being identified.

Sassy kept her head down while she worked and listened to the ladies gossiping amongst themselves. Every now and then, she interjected an 'oh, really?' or 'isn't that horrible' which seemed to satisfy everyone that she was part of their conversation.

Only Gus' image from the photo Donnelly had shown her was being circulated in the media, and not the full image, she assumed out of privacy for the yet unidentified woman. Still, no one in the village recognized him.

Going by what the media was reporting, they were now looking at this crime as a body dump, or that Gus had been taken to the riverside with the sole intention of killing him and leaving him to be found by locals.

Or an innocent, lone jogger and her dog.

Thank God, her name remained out of the news.

After the salon had closed Saturday, Sassy worked late into the night, giving the place a deep scrub. Something she couldn't identify was eating away at her insides and only hard graft kept the feelings away.

Sunday had been the worst. Despite her exhaustion from the previous full day's work and a long night of cleaning, Sassy found herself sitting up in bed as the sun was coming up. This time of year meant that was early—very early.

Unable to force herself back to sleep, or even get comfortable so she could have a long morning reading in bed, she was up and on the beach with Bracken for their morning run. The thought of her usual loop run to Mornington made her stomach hurt, so they'd been going the other direction, to Laytown. The loop was half a mile shorter, but she could live with that.

Being home and alone was usually peaceful for her. Especially after a long, busy week. She loved lazy Sundays where she could lounge around in her pajamas, dress when she wished . . . if she wished . . . and catch up on programs she'd recorded during the week. Sundays were not uncommon days for back-to-back episodes of all her favorite crime dramas.

Not this Sunday. That thing inside her forced her out onto the beach more than once for a run.

By the time evening came, Sassy had been so wound up, she was ready for another beach sprint to Laytown. When she had gone looking for Bracken, she had found the dog in the bedroom with her head under the bed, as if burying her head like an ostrich meant the rest of her lumbering body was invisible too. Not even bouncing a ball or squeaking a toy got the dog out from under the bed.

Sassy had to laugh at the situation. Their morning run was about waking up, getting the blood pumping, fresh air. The evening romp was less about exercise and more about unwinding and getting some fresh air.

But Sunday, she'd broken the routine. After their morning run, a second run was less energetic and more about play for Bracken. The third run, the dog was weary. Sassy saw it. But a fourth run? The dog told her by her refusal to budge from under the bed that enough was enough. The dog was probably right, but with that thing twisting inside her, she had decided the kitchen and bathroom needed cleaning too.

Even as night finally came, she tossed and turned, unable to figure out why.

And now she was down in the salon, looking around for something to do before the salon opened.

Sassy was going through petty cash receipts when she heard the front door open.

"You're in early," Mary chirped as she slung her coat over a peg in the hall leading to the kitchen.

"Just setting up for the day. It's going to be another busy one," she replied, hoping she sounded as chipper as Mary looked.

"By the looks of the place," Mary said, looking around the sparkling shop, "you've been doing more than just setting up." Facing Sassy, she added, "You look like hell."

"Thanks. I appreciate that. I've worked really hard to achieve this look. I'm glad it shows." She spun on her heel and went into the kitchen to fill the kettle and make sure there were clean cups for her customers. She knew they sparkled, like the rest of the salon, but it was something to do to avoid arguing with her friend.

Mary was behind her when Sassy turned to set a tray on the table for the cups. "Jazus," she exclaimed, her heart suddenly pounding and her breath caught in her throat. "You scared me." She stepped around Mary and set the tray on the table then put the cups onto it.

"Are you all right, Sass?"

She couldn't look at her friend. She was angry Mary had rung Liam behind her back about the altercation with Fiona. Or was she? They'd worked together on Saturday, and it was business as usual between the longtime pals. So why was she angry with her today?

Besides, she suspected it was Liam's option A that had Mary ringing him. Mary never said anything, but Sassy could tell by the way Mary acted around Liam that she had a little thing for him. Why she'd never come right out and said so, Sassy would never know. Unless she asked her.

To avoid talking about her weekend, she did just that.

"I hear you rang Liam." She moved back to the counter and filled the little jugs with milk she'd taken from the fridge, then took them to the table and set them beside the tray. She moved the cups from the tray onto the table, then went back to the counter.

When Mary didn't say anything, Sassy glanced over to see her friend standing with her arms crossed and a guilty look on her face. Her friend just had her best interests at heart so she wasn't going to torture her about it. Instead, to avoid an altercation about Mary butting into her business, she said, "He reckons you have a crush on him."

Mary gasped. "What— But— I mean—"

"I told him he was probably right."

"Sassy!"

Casually, Sassy took small ceramic containers filled with packets of sugar and sugar substitute to the table and set them on the tray. She moved the cups onto the tray and went back to the counter.

She pulled coffee grounds down from the cupboard and set the packet beside the kettle for when she was ready to make the coffee. "Well, you do, don't you?" She glanced up at her friend again before walking over to the table. She moved the cups onto the table, and set the containers of sugar beside them.

She looked around the kitchen. What was she missing? Oh, right. Biscuits. "I should make some fresh biscuits, don't you think?"

"Sassy, stop." Mary stayed her with a hand on Sassy's arm.

"What? Probably too much, right? Packet biscuits are good enough." When she tried moving away, Mary's hand held her firmer in place. "What?"

"How many times are you going to put the cups on the

tray and take them off?"

What was she on about? "They're on the tray? See?" When she looked over, the cups were back on the table again, beside milk and sugar she didn't remember putting out. "What the—"

Mary guided her to a chair and sat her in it. "I'll make you a coffee. Then we're talking."

For the next hour, Sassy told her friend about her meeting with Donnelly on Friday, Gus' identification, and the woman in the photo. She also told her about Donnelly's misunderstanding about Liam, and about what she felt was developing between her and the detective.

"Do I need to make another call to Liam about this, or should I ring Detective Donnelly? Either one should really help clear things up."

"I doubt it. And no you shouldn't. If you want to talk with my brother, just ring him and ask him out." Mary hesitated. "It's the twenty-first century. You don't have to wait for him to ask you."

Mary shook her head. "I don't think he even likes me . . . like that. Anyway, he probably thinks of me like a sister."

"I got the impression he enjoyed talking with you the other night." Mary's eyes widened with surprise. "Go on. Give him a ring . . ." She heard the salon door open and shot a glance at the wall clock. ". . . later, on your break."

When Sassy returned from her short lunch break, the salon was still full of customers. She had four work stations, and each of them had a customer having something done with their hair. The nail station also had a customer. Everyone was busy chatting away. She loved seeing the salon so busy.

Just as Mary was moving Mrs. Brady to the nail station, the door opened. Mary greeted the young woman and showed her to the newly freed workstation.

As Mary tidied up from Mrs. Brady's trim, Sassy gazed at the woman in the chair. Something familiar rang loudly.

What was it?

When Mary stepped into the back room where they prepared the dyes, Sassy followed. "Who is that woman in your chair?"

Mary gazed quickly through the door then went back to her preparations. "That's Ina Walsh."

"I don't remember seeing her here before. Is she new?"

"No, but recently, she's been coming in for the platinum dye. She's been away for a couple weeks. The salon she went to for a touch up told her the color was the platinum shade she wanted but it turned out too dark. So she's back for the real deal, as she said." Mary reached over for her bottle of water and took a sip. "Why do you ask?"

"She looks familiar but I can't place her, is all." Then it struck her. "What brand are we using on her today?"

Mary set the bottle aside and picked up the bowl of prepared dye and the brush she'd use to apply it to the woman's hair. Just before she left the room, she said, "Starlet, Platinum Bombshell."

Sassy shook. *Stay calm. It's probably not her.* She grabbed her mobile off the counter beside the register and brought up Donnelly's mobile number to text him.

The photo of Gus and the woman . . . send me her picture. NOW.

If she could have made the NOW bigger, she would have. She prayed he had his mobile on him. As the seconds ticked by, it seemed like hours before she heard the message waiting signal.

She went to message mode and opened the app. *What's up?* he asked, but he'd attached the close up image of the woman's face.

Ignoring his question, she tried walking as casually as possible to the opposite side of the salon. She gazed out the window and saw Fiona stomping away from Chutney, an angry look on her face. When she saw Sassy looking at her, Fiona gifted her with a raised middle finger.

She couldn't think about Fiona right now, so she faced the salon again. Lifting her phone before her, she acted like she was checking her email.

She pulled up Donnelly's image and glanced over the top of the phone at the woman in Mary's chair. It was a rough image. The original photo hadn't been a large one, and the close up image was a bit blurry, but the eyes . . . the eyes were the same. The mouth and nose . . . the same. Hair color could change, and obviously had.

She pulled up the text app and replied to Donnelly. *Ina Walsh. Get someone to look her up, but get your ass over here yesterday.*

Chapter Sixteen

"Sassy Cuts. How may I help?" She'd seen Donnelly's number come up on caller ID and answered as casually as she could. She moved down the hallway to the kitchen, closing the door softly. "What are you doing ringing me? Get over here. That woman from the photo with Gus, she's in my salon."

There was no disguising the surprise in the detective's voice. "Are you sure?"

"Do you think I'd text you like this for no reason?" Her voice hitched up a notch with annoyance.

"Well, I could hope."

"Please," she implored, "just get over here. She's your missing link. Her hair color is different from the photo, but it's the same face. I'm sure of it."

There was rustling on Donnelly's end of the phone, then he was standing outside the kitchen window in the drive.

"Jesus, Mary, and Joseph, Donnelly, you scared the crap out of me," she exclaimed, staring him down through the glass.

"Do you want to rail at me on the phone or unlock the door and let me in?"

She had it in her head to give him a piece of her mind, but after the weekend she'd had, she didn't think she could spare any more brain cells. She disconnected the call and opened the door, forcibly pulling him inside.

"How did you get here so quickly?"

"I was already on the road. I had some other local business

so I diverted here before going back to the incident room in Laytown."

"You could have told me."

"So, where is she?"

"She's upstairs, giving Bracken a bath. Where the bloody hell do you think she is?"

As quietly as possible, she opened the kitchen door and led him through the short hall toward the salon. She stopped just as Mary's work station came into view. Ina's face was a visible reflection in the mirror.

To her surprise, Ina was in tears. Mary had said she received a bad dye job, which was obvious, but she didn't think it was anything to cry over.

"Please ask Mary to join us in the kitchen." Sassy nodded at his request and returned a moment later with the woman in tow, closing the door softly behind them.

"This is Detective Donnelly, Mary." Donnelly had been in the salon before, so she didn't know why she was introducing him.

Mary rolled her eyes, apparently the same thought going through her mind. "Good morning, detective."

"Thanks for coming back here. Tell me about the woman in your chair. Miss O'Brien said her name is Ina Walsh. Is that correct?"

Mary gave Sassy a look when she replied, "Miss O'Brien, is it?" She tried, unsuccessfully in Sassy's opinion, to hide her mirth. Gazing back at Donnelly, she said, "Yes. She's been a customer here, off and on, for about a year. Why do you ask?"

Before Donnelly could speak, Sassy blurted out, "We have reason to believe she's a person of interest in the murder of Gustav Kozlow."

Both Donnelly and Mary's gazes fell heavily on her. "I'm right, aren't I . . . Detective?"

He jerked his head in the affirmative. "Yeah, and it sounded pretty good too. But how about we let me lead *my* investigation?"

Sassy held up her palms before her and stepped back.

"What Miss O'Brien said." Donnelly emphasized the miss, probably making it clear this was an official enquiry. He took out his notebook. "For the record, may I have your full name, please?"

"Sure. Is your page wide enough?" When Donnelly lifted an eyebrow at her, she said, "Mary Elizabeth Margaret Jude O'Shea."

Donnelly grunted. "Right. Mary O'Shea." He looked back at Mary and continued making notes as they spoke. "Ina Walsh, and she's been a customer here for a year." Mary nodded. "Grand. What else can you tell me about her?"

"Tell her about the bad hair job," Sassy blurted. She made the motion to zip her lips and throw away the key at the look Donnelly gave her.

"Well, she's in to have her hair dyed, like most do. She went to visit family recently and while she was there, she needed a touch up. The place she went assured her they had her color, but obviously lied to her."

"How do you know they lied?"

"She wanted platinum blonde but they gave her platinum silver."

"What's the difference? Isn't one platinum the same as another?"

Both women laughed. "Umm, no," Mary said. "Platinum silver is, well, silver or grey toned. Platinum blonde is a specific shade of blonde that's nearly white. Think Jean Harlow or Marilyn Monroe. This woman's hair had definitely been grey when she walked through the door."

Donnelly's spine noticeably straightened. "And she normally comes to this salon for her treatment?" When Mary nodded, he asked, "What brand does she normally use?"

"Same as always. Starlet, Platinum Bombshell."

Silence fell heavily in the room as the detective made notes. Sassy bounced on the balls of her feet. She wanted to run again, just to expel some pent up energy.

"What's this all about, Detective?" Mary finally asked.

"Do you know why she's crying?"

Sassy stepped closer.

"She just broke up with her fiancé."

"How long ago was this? Recently?"

Mary shook her head. "Not sure. She just said they broke up and she went to her mother's to get her head together. How is she involved with the murdered guy?

Sassy held up her phone and showed her friend the photo Donnelly had sent her a short time ago. "Do you think this is her?" Sassy asked.

Mary nodded. "Yes, absolutely. This was before she went blonde about six months ago. Do I need to be worried?"

Donnelly shook his head. "No, she's just someone of interest."

Sassy flicked a glance at the detective. "We think she was seeing the victim."

Mary's hand shot to her mouth. "I don't believe it. Are you sure?"

He shook his head yes. "When will it be possible to speak with her? I noticed she's got dye in her hair now."

"It's setting now. Takes about half an hour, which is why I'm not rushing back out there. I told her I was making her some tea, so maybe I should do that and take it out?"

"Absolutely. How long until you're done? We need to speak with her, but I don't want to upset her mid-treatment."

"Can you give me forty minutes?"

He nodded, and added, when he noticed her hands were shaking, "Please, keep this conversation to yourself. The news will be a shock to her, so stay calm and act normal."

"I'll do my best." Mary prepared a quick cup of tea and grabbed a small plate and put some biscuits on it before returning to the salon.

When she had gone, Sassy turned to Donnelly. "This is going to be the longest forty minutes of my life."

Chapter Seventeen

Ina appeared in the kitchen doorway forty-five minutes later. Her hair was now a glossy platinum blonde which fell about her shoulders. A concerned look etched her pretty features.

Mary stepped around her and closed the door.

Both Sassy and Donnelly rose from the table to greet her.

While they waited, Donnelly had a chat with Sassy about letting him lead the enquiry with Ina, promising he would put her out of the room if she interfered. The questioning really should be carried out at the station, but as he was treating this as a notification of death rather than a murder enquiry, it could be done more casually. But Sassy had to stay out of it. She promised.

"Thanks, Mary," Donnelly said. "I'll take it from here."

When Mary reluctantly left, Sassy offered Ina a cup of tea. "No, thank you. I just had one. What's this about?"

Donnelly motioned for her to sit, and when she did, he sat across from her. Sassy sat away from them at the opposite end of the table.

"I'm Detective Donnelly. Are you Ina Walsh?" When Ina nodded, he continued. "What's your permanent local address?" She quickly recited her address in Bettystown. He then pulled out the photo his team had found in Gus' caravan in Clogherhead. "Is this you with Gustav Kozlow?"

Ina started shaking noticeably. "What is this about?"

"Is this you?" he repeated.

"Yes. That's me and Gus. Why?"

"When was the last time you saw Gus?"

Ina's brows drew together. "I don't know. About two weeks I think. Why? Has something happened to him?"

Donnelly took a deep breath. "I'm afraid I have some bad news."

Tears rolled down Ina's already red eyes. "He's dead, isn't he?" A sob jerked free from her throat.

Donnelly nodded. "His remains were recently identified. We believe he was killed two weeks ago. You may have been the last person to see him alive. We've been looking for you since we discovered this photo in his caravan."

Ina took the photo in her shaking fingers and looked at it. She ran a fingertip over Gus' face before pushing the image aside and buried her face in her hands and sobbed.

Sassy rose for a box of tissues on the old china dresser in the corner and placed them in front of Ina, along with a glass of water. Donnelly had told her to stay quiet, and she was. It didn't mean she couldn't offer the woman some comfort. She pulled a few tissues from the box and put them into Ina's hand before sitting down again.

Ina mouthed her thanks. "How do you know I was the last person to see him alive?"

"Forensics showed he had some platinum-blonde hairs in his hand."

"How do you know they're mine?" she asked.

"Well, we don't, but as Miss O'Brien has told us, she's the only salon in the east selling the brand of dye you use. Your name came up on a short list of customers who use the same product. We were making our way around to speaking with you. Miss O'Brien recognized you from the photo of the victim—"

"You mean Gus."

"Yes, sorry, Gus. She recognized you from the photo and rang me to come talk with you now. I'm sorry we have to meet under such difficult circumstances. I'm sorry for your loss," he added.

Ina blew her nose into the tissues and pulled a few more from the box. "Well, what do you need to know?"

Donnelly gazed into Ina's eyes, his expression one of concern, but also wanting just the facts.

"There's not much to tell. Where do I start?"

"The beginning is usually best. How did you meet?"

"In a nightclub in Drogheda. About a year ago. I never considered dating a Polish guy before, but he was really sweet. Much quieter than other guys, you know? Anyway, we danced a little, talked a little. Promised to meet the next weekend. It went on from there. I wasn't really interested in dating him, since he spent so much time out at sea, but we promised to try making it work. I thought it was working. He proposed to me at the carnival." she glanced at the photo still laying before her. "This picture was taken not long after. I was so happy."

"What happened?" he asked.

"Not long after the carnival, I had my hair dyed. Just for fun. He didn't like it though. Said it made him feel unfaithful to me. He ordered me to change it back and I refused. We fought over it a few times."

"Is that why you broke up?"

She nodded. "Part of the reason. Guys just don't order women around anymore. Anyway, he said he was sorry and asked to meet me. He wanted to make it up to me. So we met over at Maiden Tower. We loved that spot. It's so romantic."

Donnelly cast a quick look Sassy's direction before continuing. "Is that where you last saw Gus?" Ina nodded. "Tell me about it. What happened?"

"Gus was already there when I arrived. A friend dropped me off. We were going to walk back to town. We hadn't seen each other for about a month, since the boat was out for so long that trip." She blushed then. "I'm embarrassed to admit it without sounding like some Mills & Boon drama queen, but I flung myself at him. I missed him so much. We kissed for a long time, but . . ."

They waited for her to continue. Sassy nearly forgot her promise, wanting to ask Ina to hurry with her story.

Finally she said, "Then he pushed me away. He said he thought he could get used to me with blonde hair, but it reminded him too much of the girl he left in Poland. He demanded I change it again and become me again. When I refused, he pushed me away. I got angry and told him if he couldn't accept me, regardless of my hair color, then we were done. I threw my ring at him and walked away. That's the last time I saw him."

Sassy watched Donnelly furiously trying to keep up with notes as Ina spoke. When he finished, he gazed up at Ina. "Nothing else happened? He was alive when you left him at the tower?"

Ina quickly nodded. "Tell me, detective, was he found at the tower?" When he nodded yes, Ina sobbed again. "Do you think one of us was followed there? Could I have been killed too?"

"We don't know, Miss Walsh. We're still putting the clues together. But knowing he was seeing someone and then finding the photo of you two together, we've been looking for you to ask what you may know."

"That's all I know."

"How do you think Gus came to have strands of your hair in his hand?"

Sassy's leg started bouncing under the table with agitation. She crossed her legs to stop it and folded her arms in front of her to help stop her heart from pounding. Why did witness questioning never take this long on Castle? The wait was killing her. She cringed at her choice of words.

"I don't know. Maybe while we were kissing? He put his hands through my hair just before he pushed me away. Oh, and when I turned to leave him, he grabbed me. He pulled my hair. I thought he was mad and coming after me so I ran. I didn't even look back. I was so upset."

Donnelly scribbled more notes.

"The ring," he said, looking up at her. "What happened to the ring? You said you threw it at him."

"I don't know what happened to it. I threw it at him. I assume he caught it. At the time, I really didn't care."

Donnelly pulled some papers from the file he'd taken the photo from. Among the papers were more photographs. He chose one Sassy recognized as the ring she'd found in the stones.

"Is this the ring?" he asked. She nodded.

Ina started tearing bits off the tissue in her hands. She was clearly upset about this. As much as she tried acting like her break up hadn't mattered, knowing Gus had been killed had hit her hard. Why wouldn't it? They were to spend the rest of their lives together. Until that night.

Sassy watched Ina fidgeting with the tissue. It looked like snow had fallen on the table.

Then blood. Just a few drops, but blood just the same.

"Detective," she said, as calmly as possible. When he glanced over, she motioned to her finger then flicked a glance in Ina's direction. When he saw what she was motioning to, he went through his photos again until he found one of the piece of plastic they'd found in the dried blood on the collar. It had tested for the same acrylic used in making false nails, and the color was a generic brand found where most nail products were sold.

"Miss Walsh. Please tell me, how did you hurt yourself?" he asked calmly.

"What? I—oh . . . I don't know. I broke a nail a while back and didn't notice until it started hurting. It broke off down into the skin. I got fake nails to help me stop chewing my own ones, but it hasn't helped. Since I couldn't have it repaired like that, I just cut them all off. I still keep worrying it, so it hasn't healed yet." She looked at the mess she'd made of the tissues on the table. "I'm sorry. I'll throw these away when we're done here."

Sassy smiled tightly and waved away the woman's promise,

as if to say it was okay and not to worry.

Donnelly replaced all the photos and documents into his folder and closed his notebook. Then he looked up at Ina. "Miss Walsh, this meeting began as an unfortunate notification of death."

"I know. I appreciate it, even though Gus and I were no longer together. I mean, since we had broken up before this happened to him. I wish I could go back and end things more amicably with him. If I had known that was the last thing he'd know before he—" She broke down in tears again.

"I know. But with the new information you have provided, I'd like to take you into Laytown for a formal statement. You were the last person to see Gus alive, and I think it's important you put this information down on the record. Will you go with me?"

Ina nodded. "Anything to help catch Gus' killer."

Donnelly stood and pulled Ina's chair out for her to rise.

"Miss O'Brien, would you mind grabbing the folder for me—" he flicked his gaze at the bloodied tissues still on the table, indicating he wanted those too, "—and follow us out to the car?"

Chapter Eighteen

"Do you think Ina knows she may have killed Gus?" Sassy asked Donnelly, when he returned later that evening. They sat on the sofa in her sitting room, their coffee going cold on the table in front of them.

She was happy Bracken hadn't barked the house down when she saw Donnelly in the kitchen. He'd arrived up the back steps since the salon was long closed. He was becoming such a common sight in her flat, it appeared Bracken now treated him as a friend. She was sure the biscuits and playing on the beach last Friday helped.

The dog now lay on her giant bed in the corner with her head down, but watching them with sleepy eyes.

"I doubt it," Donnelly said. "Ina consented to some tests, but we won't know for sure until we get the DNA results back. I'm pretty sure they'll match."

"What do you think happened out there . . . with Gus and Ina?"

"I can't really discuss it with you."

She gave him a look that said Oh, really? "After everything we've been through together the last two weeks, you're going to try playing that card with me?"

He gazed seriously at her for a long moment before he chuckled. "I suppose I can't. Okay, it's purely conjecture, but I think this was an accident. She probably unknowingly stabbed him with her fake nail while they argued. What are the odds of something like that happening?"

"Acrylic nails are stronger than you think. It was just pure, dumb luck she managed to hit an artery."

Donnelly gestured his agreement with a nod.

"What about the hair?"

"The hair probably stuck to his fingers while they were kissing, as she said, or he could have gotten them when he pulled them as she was leaving. When she thinks he pulled her hair, he could have been grasping for her to come back because he was hurt. Blood on the one hand was probably him trying to stop the bleeding. Hair in the other hand was him reaching out to stop her. Since she said she never looked back, she didn't know he was hurt. Given the timeline she gave us down at the station, she probably wouldn't have even seen the blood on him. The sun was already down."

"And the ring?"

"He probably never caught it. Again, given the time, he might not have even seen her throw it."

How tragically it all had played out. A stupid argument, a proud man, a stubborn woman, misunderstanding, anger . . . an accidental death that will surely haunt poor Ina the rest of her life.

"So, all the evidence leads to Ina. Do you think they'll charge her with murder?"

"No. Murder is premeditated. Didn't your crime shows teach you anything?" He dramatically rolled his eyes, but there was humor in them and she gave his leg a shove with her bare foot.

"What about manslaughter? I know that's not premeditated, but it comes in degrees. Manslaughter is causing an unintentional death, right?"

"Right, but it usually stems from criminal intent."

"There wasn't any criminal intent involved here."

"No, there wasn't, but involuntary manslaughter also includes reckless behavior," he told her.

"But she wasn't behaving recklessly. It wasn't like she was goading him to swim across the Boyne and he drowned."

Donnelly chuckled. "True."

94

When he gazed at her, his eyes lit with humor. It felt good—natural—sitting here with him like this in her place. Easy discussion of a quiet evening, and the calmness that had settled around them once they'd heard Ida's story. She found she quite liked this.

She liked *him*.

And he seemed to like her. She liked that too.

But now that the case was effectively closed, he'd be returning to Ashbourne. While Ashbourne wasn't that far away—just a forty-five minute drive—it was like another world to the one here on the coast.

Sadness filled her, and she gazed away.

Was this it? Was this the last time she'd see Detective Donnelly? Hell, she didn't even know his first name. Come to think of it, he'd never called her Sassy either. They never really were formally introduced.

"Hey," he said, drawing her attention. "You all right?"

She hesitantly nodded. "Grand, why?"

"You looked very sad there for a moment. Sad about your case wrapping up . . . *Detective* O'Brien?" He winked, but she didn't find much humor in it.

She pushed him again with her foot. Then bringing her knees up in front of her, she cradled them in her arms. "Very funny," she said. "I'm just glad Gus' story was told, and Ina will probably be vindicated. It was a horrible accident that shouldn't have happened."

Donnelly waved his hand in her direction. "Is that what this is all about? You're sad for this couple?"

She shrugged. "Maybe. I don't know. It all just seems so pointless."

"I couldn't agree more. But people do all kinds of crazy things for love."

She supposed so.

"Have you ever done anything crazy for love?"

Chapter Nineteen

She slowly gazed up at him. She didn't want to talk about her love life, not that she had one. She certainly didn't want to tell him about Seamus. But now that there didn't seem to be anything else to distract them, they better have the talk about Liam before he left for home.

"Listen, we need to have that talk, Donnelly. You never did ring me Saturday like you promised, but I understand—the case came first. Now that it's all over, I think you and I need to clear the air. Especially as you're heading back to Ashbourne."

Donnelly turned toward her fully, resting his bent knee across the cushion between them, and flung his elbow across the back of the sofa. "I'm sorry for not contacting you. You're right, the case took up a lot of my time. But I'm here now. We can talk about whatever you want."

She released a pent up breath. Now that she had his undivided attention, she didn't know where to start. What did he say to Ina . . . at the beginning?

"So . . . you know that man up in Clogherhead?"

"You mean your brother, Liam, in Port Oriel?"

She shot her gaze up at him.

"What the hell, Donnelly? You knew?"

"Of course I did. What kind of detective would I be if I didn't investigate every clue and every suspect we had?" He gave her a cheeky grin.

"Why didn't you tell me you knew?"

"Why didn't you tell me sooner?"

He had a point. They'd been playing with each other. No wonder he felt so free to touch her all those times. He must know she was attracted to him, and she was sure every continued touch and every inappropriate time he gazed at her was meant to endear him more and more in her heart. Had he succeeded?

"You're a cheeky cad. You know that though, don't you? Ha! Look at that grin. Of course you do."

Donnelly chuckled again. "Is there anything else you want to tell me, or was that it?"

She thought about Seamus. He probably already knew about him too. "No, I don't think there's anything I need to tell you at this juncture."

"What do you mean this juncture?"

"Well . . . you're leaving for Ashbourne. Your business here is done, right?"

"My official business is, why?"

"What do you mean official business?"

"I have personal business that needs my attention."

Curiosity ate at her but she wasn't going to pry. Much. "Does that mean you'll be around for a couple days then?" She hoped.

"Probably."

"Really?" She couldn't keep her surprise from showing.

"You'll find out soon enough. I have family in Bettystown, so you'll be seeing more of me around."

The news stole the words from her mouth. Whatever she thought he was going to say, it certainly wasn't that. She opened her mouth to speak and closed it. Then tried and failed again.

Donnelly laughed. "I can't believe it. The spunky Miss O'Brien is suddenly lost for words."

She chuffed. "Well, yeah. I mean . . .Why didn't you tell me earlier?"

He shrugged. "Why didn't you tell me about Liam?"

She narrowed her gaze at him. "Do I know your family?

I'm sure I do. I mean, you know how village life is."

"You know my grandmother very well, actually. Honora Ellison. Most people just call her Nora though."

Sassy mind spun. The customer she'd stood up the day she'd found Gus' body had to be his grandmother. Of all the women in Bettystown, Mrs. Ellison had to be his grandmother. Sassy felt like crying, but laughed instead at the irony of it.

"She hates me, you know."

"I don't believe it. Why would she hate you? She tells me you're the only one she allows to cut and color her hair."

"Really?" she squeaked out.

"She was angry when you left her waiting that morning, but when I found out it was you, I explained everything to her," he said.

She had wondered why Mrs. Ellison had unexpectedly returned to her salon last week. Sassy was sure she'd never see the woman again. And the woman had asked her to personally handle her appointment. She must have gotten over her anger at being stood up. Now she understood.

And Sassy understood why she'd moved to Bettystown, even though she kept talking about her home in England. She moved to be closer to her grandson—Detective Donnelly.

Sassy was about ready to tell him what a sweet grandson he was and how he must really love his grandmother when a realization hit her. The retired police inspector's wife he'd mentioned having been in the supermarket the day Fiona confronted her must have been Mrs. Ellison. Sassy had greeted her as she left the store but she'd forgotten all about it.

"Does your grandmother call you Detective Donnelly too, or is that just me?"

"Lots of people call me that, why?"

"I just realized I've only ever called you by your surname. The business card you gave me just says Detective F. Donnelly. What the hell does the F. stand for?"

"Finn."

"Hmm . . ." she muttered, looking him up and down. "Suits you. Finn Donnelly." She liked how Finn sounded when she said his name aloud.

"So, are all our cards on the table now?"

She thought for a moment. "I suppose they are, except for one thing."

"What's that?"

"You have to stop calling me Miss O'Brien."

Finn chuckled. "What do I call you then? Do you prefer Saoirse or Sassy?"

Sassy gasped. He really had done his homework. When they were children, Liam couldn't say Saoirse when he was learning to speak. Sassy was the closest he could manage. It suited her, so it had stuck.

"I'm Sassy."

Without missing a beat, Finn said, "Yes. Yes, you are."

ABOUT KEMBERLEE SHORTLAND

Kemberlee was born and raised in Northern California in an area known as America's Salad Bowl. It was home to many authors, including John Steinbeck, and for a while Jack London and Robert Louis Stevenson.

In 1997, Kemberlee left the employ of Clint Eastwood when the opportunity to live in Ireland for six months presented itself. It was there she ended up meeting a man who convinced her to stay. Kemberlee is now celebrating her eighteenth year in Ireland and has been lucky to travel the country extensively, picking up a cupla focal along the way—a few Irish words.

Kemberlee has been writing since a very young age and over the years she has published dozens of travel articles and book reviews, as well as worked with some notable authors who've set their books in Ireland.

2006 saw the publication of Kemberlee's first two short stories, Tutti-Frutti Blues and Dude Looks Like a Lady, set in her hometown. Since then, Kemberlee has published a number of short stories and novels, many of which are set in Ireland.

Kemberlee currently lives in Mornington, Ireland with her husband and dog-child.

GET IN TOUCH WITH KEMBERLEE

Author Website
www.kemberlee.com

Facebook
www.facebook.com/AuthorKemberleeShortland

Twitter
www.twitter.com/kemberlee

LinkedIn
www.linkedin.com/in/kemberlee

Heart Shaped Stones
www.heartshapedstones.blogspot.com

Hearticles: Articles with Heart
www.hearticles.blogspot.com

Tirgearr Publishing
www.tirgearrpublishing.com/authors/Shortland_Kemberlee

BOOKS BY KEMBERLEE

Irish Pride Series
Rhythm Of My Heart, #1
A Piece Of My Heart, #2
Shape Of My Heart, #3

The Carmel Charmers Series
Tutti-Frutti Blues
Dude Looks Like A Lady

City Nights Series
One Night In Dublin

ABCs Of S-E-X: Love By The Letter Series
Awakening, #1

Stand-Alone Books
The Power Of Love
Moondance

IRISH PRIDE SERIES

RHYTHM OF MY HEART, #1
ISBN (ebook): 9781476474540
ISBN (print): 9781910234037

Eilis Kennedy, gave up a singing career to become an Artists Representative with Eireann Records. Kieran Vaughan is just the talent she needs to contract who will really launch her career, while at the same time getting her out from under her boss's thumb. Fergus Manley vows to have Eilis in his bed at any cost.

A PIECE OF MY HEART, #2
ISBN (ebook): 9781311400499
ISBN (print): 9781910234051

Ten years after their break-up, the addendum in Mick's father's will forces Mick and Kate together to save Mick's heritage. Kate thought she was falling in love with Mick all over again, but a new revelation is too much for her. She is determined to finally say goodbye forever to her childhood sweetheart. Mick has other plans for Kate's future. And none of them involve goodbye.

SHAPE OF MY HEART, #3
ISBN (ebook): 9781310788833
ISBN (print): 9781910234044

Gráinne moonlights at The Klub! to earn money for college tuition. John 'JD' Desmond is an undercover detective. The Klub!, owned by Jimmy Malloy, is being used as a drug front, headed by the notorious Taylor 'The Hunter' Wade. JD wanted Gráinne to snitch for him, but things get complicated when they fall in love. When Gráinne witnesses Jimmy's murder, she and JD are forced to run for their lives.

THE CARMEL CHARMERS SERIES
ISBN: 97811466131453

The Carmel Charmers Series includes the novelettes Tutti-Frutti Blues and Dude Looks Like A Lady. These stories are set in the quaint town of Carmel-by-the-Sea, California, when eating ice cream while walking through town was illegal and one required a permit to wear high heels!

TUTTI-FRUTTI BLUES
ISBN: 9781465873644

Town therapist Maisie Daniels is having a bad day. A double scoop of tutti-frutti ice cream is sure to boost her mood. When Sgt Jake Hennessey spots her step out of the shop with her cone, he doesn't to cite her for eating ice cream on the street, a recent ban, but invites her to dinner instead. By he end of dinner, Jake thinks he could love Maisie.

DUDE LOOKS LIKE A LADY
ISBN: 9781466013766

Pamela Howard can't believe she let her friend Maisie talk her into dressing as King Louis XVI for a charity event. Hank Delacroix is ready to throttle his friend Jake for tricking him into dressing as Marie Antoinette. When Pam finally meets her partner, memories and heartache awaken. And when Hank realizes Louis is his ex-fiancé, he has to find a way to finally apologize.

CITY NIGHTS SERIES

ONE NIGHT IN DUBLIN
ISBN:9781311609366

At her mother's prompting (nagging) about grandchildren, Sive wonders if it really is time to settle down. She's just finishing college so she should be thinking about her future. But is she ready to settle down? Is she ready for kids? And more importantly, which of the three men she's been seeing does she want to spend the rest of her life with? Sive has a choice to make, and only 24 hours in which to make it.

ABCS OF S-E-X: LOVE BY THE LETTER SERIES

AWAKENING, #1
ISBN: 9781465986122

Ysbail is the ward of the Prince of Powys. Bedwyr is the bastard son of the King of Gwynedd. When a peace settlement is reached between Prince Madog and King Owain, it's at Ysbail and Bedwyr's expense. Known as the Grave Knower, war has taken Bedwyr to the edge of insanity. But when he first sees Ysbail, his blood-thirst turns to blood-lust, and vows to show Ysbail she needn't fear him.

STAND-ALONE BOOKS

THE POWER OF LOVE
ISBN: 9781301884315

When Elaine discovers she's pregnant, she hesitates telling her husband, Ethan. They're newlyweds and want to wait until they're ready to start a family. Ethan surprised her by accepting early parenthood. But when they receive bad news after a prenatal exam, both must face that their charmed lives were about to come crashing down around them. Do Christmas wishes really come true?

MOONDANCE
ISBN: 9781476167084

Blánaid thinks there's something wrong with her. She hasn't dated in months. If not for her best friends, Ronan and Siobhan, Blánaid is sure she'll go crazy with loneliness and despair. Then, one night while watching the sunset, Ronan kisses her and suddenly, Blánaid's world is thrown into turmoil. Can Blánaid face the truth in Siobhan's words? Can Ronan settle for just being Blánaid's friend?